餐飲英語

李普生 著

應用外語 05

ENGLISH

Food
Service
Industry

五南圖書出版公司 印行

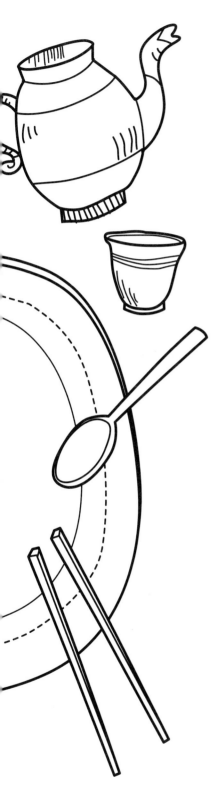

編輯說明

　　由於科技發達交通便利，餐飲的經營早已開始跨國躍進，而每年湧進台灣的上百萬觀光客及精緻或商務旅館的林立更使得餐飲服務對外（英）語能力的重依賴性與日俱增。舉凡針對餐飲服務業的專業英語或留學生到國外餐廳打工或出國旅遊時的點菜用餐等目的，一本功能明確且簡易上口的工具書尤顯重要！

本書共計 14 單元，每單元中又分成 6 節：

- 課文（Read）是與本單元主題相關的基本常識
- 詞彙（Glossary）中提供與單元名稱相關的基本用字和片語
- 進階式情境對話（What to Say）中以 4 段對話將可能的情境逐一介紹，並附加 MP3 錄音檔
- 句型介紹（How to Say It）中將在該單元出現過或與該單元相關的不同表達加以提醒
- 文法重點（Grammar Focus）中將本單元曾出現的文法觀念做提綱挈領的說明和複習
- 練習（Drills & Exercises）中以填空、代換、選擇及角色扮演等練習方式，來對於單元中所講授的內容加以練習

- 小常識（Knowledge）中幫助學習者對不同的行為表現或認知進行文化等資訊的解讀

　　除上述固定章節外，本書將於相關單元中補充並明列各式飲料菜名菜單和烹飪方法的用字，以及與餐飲相關資訊提供學習者更多有用的知識。

　　本書中所提供的資訊絕非僅有，而相關用語用法也絕非絕對；隨著資訊取得的容易和實際體驗機會的頻繁，讀者唯有不時「停看聽」才能精進、才能提升！

CONTENTS

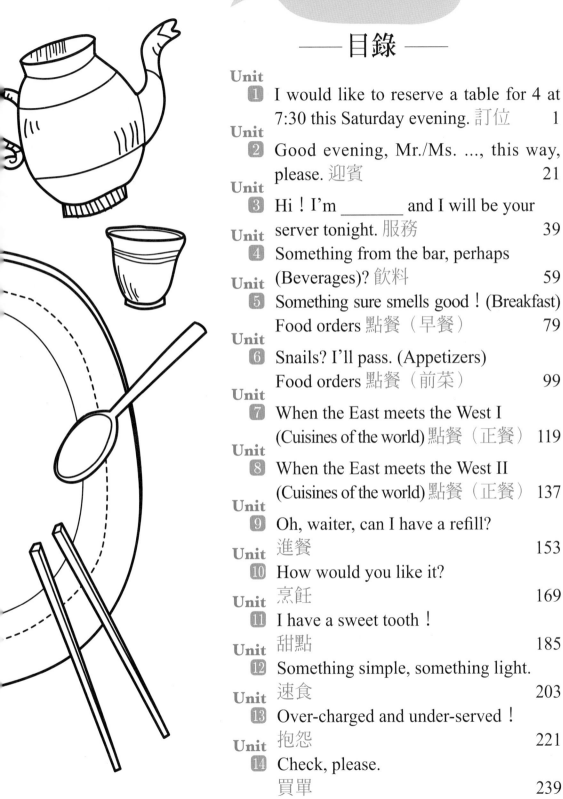

目錄

Unit

1

I would like to reserve a table for 4 at 7:30 this saturday evening. 訂位

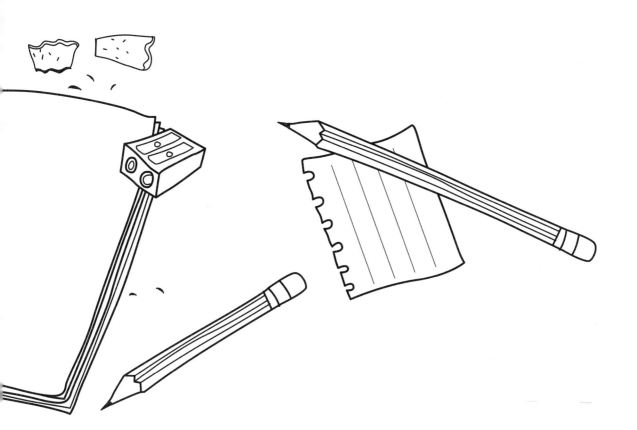

Read 閱讀

———○———

There are various types of restaurants, and they fall into several industry (行業) classifications (分類) based upon menu style, preparation methods and pricing (價位):

A Fast-food restaurant 「速食店」 emphasizes speed of service, and its operations ranging from small-scale (小規模) street vendors (街頭小販) with carts (推車) to franchised (授權連鎖經銷商) mega-corporations (大公司) like McDonald's.

In comparison, a Fast-food casual restaurant 「熱炒小吃店」 does not offer table service (桌邊服務), but may offer non-disposable (重覆使用) plates and cutlery (刀 , 餐具); the quality of food and price are higher than those of a conventional (傳統的) fast-food restaurant.

Family style restaurants 「家庭餐廳」 are restaurants that have a fixed (固定) menu and fixed price, and are usually with diners seated at a communal table (公桌 ; 所有人坐在一起).

Casual (輕鬆隨便) dining restaurant/diner「餐室 , 茶餐廳」is a restaurant that serves moderately-priced (中等價位) food in a casual atmosphere (氣氛); it typically provides table service.

Fine dining restaurants「美食餐廳」are full service restaurants with specific dedicated (專注的) meal courses. Décor (裝潢) of such restaurants features (以…為特色) higher quality materials with an eye towards (著眼於) the "atmosphere" desired by any standard.

Cafes and coffee shops「咖啡店」are informal restaurants offering a range of hot meals and made-to-order (在接單後開始烹飪) sandwiches. In some areas, cafes offer outdoor seating. A café can offer table service, but many times the guest orders at the front (櫃台), and the food is brought out to the table, Then while at most casual dining restaurants the guest pays with the server, at a café the guest most often pays with a cashier (出納).

A cafeteria「自助餐廳」is a restaurant serving mostly ready-cooked (已烹飪好的) food arranged behind a food-serving counter. There is little or no table service with a pa-

tron (客人) takes a tray (托盤) and pushes it along a track (軌道) in front of the counter.

Coffeehouses「咖啡餐廳」are casual restaurants without table service that emphasize coffee and other beverages (飲料); typically, a limited selection of cold food such as pastries (糕點) and perhaps sandwiches are offered as well. Mainly in the UK and other countries influenced by British culture, a pub (short for public house) (簡稱「酒館」) is a bar that serves simple food fare (伙食, 食物). In France, a brasserie「簡樸餐廳」/bistro「小餐廳」is a café doubling as (兼任) a restaurant and serving moderately priced hearty (豐盛的) meals, i.e. the French version (形式, 版本) of "comfort food" (慰藉食物) in a relaxed setting (環境).

All-you-can-eat buffet and smorgasbord「吃到飽自助餐」restaurant offers customers a selection of food at a fixed price. The selection can be modest (適度的) or very extensive (廣泛的), with the more elaborate (精細的) menus divided into categories such as salad, soup, appetizers (前菜), hot entrees (主食), cold entrees, and dessert and fruit.

A teppanyaki「鐵板燒」restaurant specializes in Japanese cuisine (菜餚), where patrons sit around the grill (烤架) while a chef (主廚) prepares their food orders in front of them. Often the chef is trained in entertaining the guests with special techniques, including cracking (打破) a spinning (旋轉的) egg in the air and flipping (翻轉) grilled shrimp pieces into patrons' mouths!

A Mongolian barbeque「蒙古烤肉」is a restaurant where customers create a bowl from an assortment (各式各樣的搭配) of ingredients (食材) displayed in a buffet fashion, the bowl is then handed to the cook who stir-fried (炒) the food on a large griddle (淺鍋) and returns it on a plate or in a bowl to the customer.

A destination restaurant「以品嘗美食為旅行往返目的的餐廳」is one that has a strong enough appeal (訴求) to draw customers from beyond its community (外地).

Glossary: Words you can use 詞彙

———○———

A

accept	接受
accommodate	配合，滿足
all booked up/booked (up) solid/fully booked	訂滿了
alternative	另外的選擇
an available table	空桌
an opening	有空位
a party of	一夥人，一行人
appropriate	適當，恰當
along with	和
a smoking ban	禁菸
at times	有時
attire	服裝
availability	有空位

B

beat (=avoid) the crowd	避開人潮
be out of reach	無法找到
beverage	飲料
book/reserve	預訂
booster seat/cushion	小餐椅 / 椅墊
booth	小房間，雅座
by oneself	獨自一人

C

cancel a reservation	取消訂位
casual	便服
come up	(臨時)發生
comply with/in compliance with	遵守
change of schedule	改變時/行程

D

dine	進餐
dress code	服裝要求

E

early bird	早到的人
establishment	組織，單位

F

feel like to + V-ing	想要
first come, first serve/first in, first serve	先到的先服務
flexible	有彈性
formal	正式

H

have trouble + V-ing	在…有問題

have no choice but...	不得不⋯
high chair	(幼童的)高腳椅
hold	保留
hold on	稍後
hours of operations/business hours	營業時間

I

i.e. (= that is)	換言之
in advance	事先
in one's name/under the name of	在⋯名下
infant	嬰兒
inform + 人 + of + 事	告訴某人某事
in the way	擋到了

L

look forward to +V-ing	盼望

M

major credit cards	各大主要信用卡
make a change to	改變
make an exception of	開例
make a note	註明
means	方法，方式

O

originally	本來

P

pardon	請求原諒
polite	有禮貌的
private dining area/room	私人進餐區
provide	提供
put through	接通

R

require	要求
round the clock	24 小時營業

S

sandals	涼鞋
semi-formal	半正式服飾
shorts	短褲
smoking/non-smoking area	吸菸 / 禁菸區
squeeze	擠入
suitable	適當的

T

terrace/outdoor patio	陽台 / 室外露臺
tough (luck)	困難；運氣差
24/7 (twenty-four-seven)	全年無休

W

waiting area/waiting list	等候區 / 候補名單
wheelchair access	無障礙（坡道）
would like to + V (原形)	想要

What to Say 情境對話

———○———

Situational Dialogue 1　　🔘1-1

S (Staff): Good afternoon. This is Early Bird Restaurant. How may I help you?

C (Caller): Yes, I'd like to make a dinner reservation for Saturday night.

S Yes, sir. How many people are there in your party? And what time would you like to make the reservation?

C There will be four people – two adults, one child and one infant. We'd like to make the reservation for 6.

S Very well, let me check the availability. No, I'm afraid we don't have a table available until 8:30. Would that time be suitable for you?

C That's a bit late for us, but I guess we have no choice but to take it.

S How about coming in earlier? Say, 5:30ish? You know, to beat the crowd?

C That will be great!

Situational Dialogue 2　　🔘1-2

S And which name should I put the reservation under?

C It's Jason Lee L-E-E.

S OK, that's L-E-E. Alright, Mr. Lee, for a party of four for Saturday at 5:30 p.m. Is there anything else we should know?

C Do you think it's possible for us to have a booster seat or a cushion for the young children? Also, we need a high chair as well.

S No problem, Mr. Lee. I'll make a note along with your reservation. Those should be ready when you come in. We look forward to seeing you.

C Great. Thanks a lot.

Situational Dialogue 3 1-3

H (Hostess): Double Tree Restaurant. This is Jenny speaking. How can I be of any assistance to you?

C (Caller): Hi, I was wondering, is it possible to make a reservation for 10 people tomorrow night?

H I will have to check, it might be a bit tough. OK, sir, it seems that we should be able to squeeze you in. May I have you name, please?

C Before we get into that, do you have a dress code in your establishment? Also, is it possible for us to have a private room?

H Yes, we do. Sandals and shorts are not allowed in the dining area. Other than that, we are quite flexible. As for the private dining area, yes, we will be able to accommodate you.

C OK, the name is Jason Wu and my telephone number is 2885-5574, or you can reach me on my cell at 0922-686-886.

H You are all set, Mr. Wu. See you tomorrow night.

C Hi, I called yesterday about the dinner reservation for 10 this evening.

H Yes, Mr. Wu, I remember that. So, what can I do you this time?

C Well, you see, something came up in the office and it seems that none of us would be able to make it tonight.

H That's too bad. So, what would you like us to do, Mr. Wu?

C Can I first cancel the reservation and then change it to next Friday night?

H I see no reason why you can't. So, it will be for a party of 10 for next Friday evening, am I correct?

C No, we will have 6 instead this time, and we still need a private room if we can.

H No problem, Mr. Wu. Look forward to seeing you then.

How to Say It 句型介紹

———○———

Followings are some useful expressions you can use when making and taking reservations:

- Good morning/afternoon/evening, _____ (name of the restaurant). May I help you? /What can I do for you? (寒暄，問候)

- For how many persons, please? /How many people are there is your party? / How many of you may we expect in your party? (確定人數)

- What date / Which day would you like to make the reservation? (確定日期)

- And what time will the reservation be for? When can we expect you? / When would you like to make the reservation for? (確定時間)

- Will that be smoking or non-smoking area? (吸菸 / 不吸菸)

- Which would you prefer? A table in the main dining area or a private room perhaps? (確定位置)

- Could you hold for a minute so that I can check the availability? (確定是否有位置)

- May I have your name and your telephone, please? (確定顧客相關資料)

- Could you spell your name for me, please? (確定名字的拼法)

- Is there a dress code? /Do you accept credit cards? /How about wheelchair access? / Is there a minimum charge? (詢問服裝規定 , 無障礙空間及最低消費)

- We open 24-7 (讀 成 : twenty-four-seven). / The regular business hours are from 11:30 to 2:30 for lunch and 5:30 to 10:00 for dinner. (營業時間)

- I'm sorry, but we are fully booked at that time. Would you mind changing your time? /I'm afraid the next available table will be at _____. Will that be OK? / I can't guarantee a table _____ (e.g. by the window, in the center,

close to the bar,…), I'll see what we can do. (因客滿而提供其他選擇)

- Since we have a very long waiting list, we can only hold your reservation for an extra 15 minutes. (告知訂位保留的限制)

- We would appreciate it if you call us in advance if you will be unable to make it. (訂位取消的規定)

- I would like to cancel my reservation. /I would like to change my reservation to another date/time if I can. (改變訂位時間)

- Thank you for calling us and we look forward to seeing you soon. / We'll be expecting you. / Looking forward to having you with us. (感謝顧客惠顧)

Note

Grammar Focus 文法重點

———○———

在本單元的閱讀（Read）中出現了下列的敘述：

"… the quality of food and price are higher than *those* of a conventional restaurant."

其中以斜體字所標示出的 those 實際上是一種與指示代名詞相關的文法應用：

「this 和 that 代替前面已提及的句子或子句，

　that 和 those 代替前面已說過的名詞，

　this 代替後者：that 代替前者」

▶ The diner was newly decorated, and this makes it a trendy place.
這餐室新裝潢過，而新裝潢這件事讓它成為一個時髦的地方。

▶ The Applebees just announced a 25% price hike; but that doesn't seem to scare the patrons away.
Applebees 餐廳剛剛宣布價位調漲 25%，但調漲價位那件事似乎並沒把客人嚇走。

▶ The ingredient in this restaurant is different from that in other restaurant.
這家餐廳用的食材和那家用的不同。

▶ The services in some small restaurants are sometimes far better than those in fancy ones.
小餐廳的服務有時比高級餐廳來得更好。

▶ Health is above wealth for this can't give us so much happiness as that.
健康比財富重要，因後者無法帶來和前者般的快樂。

尤其是在代替先前已說過的名詞時，更要小心，因為英文文法中明確指出不相同事物之間無法比較。

The climate in Taiwan is much milder than Japan. (✗)
The climate in Taiwan is much milder than that in Japan. (○)

"Those (who)" 通常指「人」。

Those (who) are interested in the coming outing, sign up by Friday.
對即將來臨的出遊感興趣的人在周五前報名。

Drills & Exercises

—— 練習 ——

Work with a partner and take turns being a staff and a caller using the words and phrases you learned in this unit by following the patterns below to conduct a conversation:

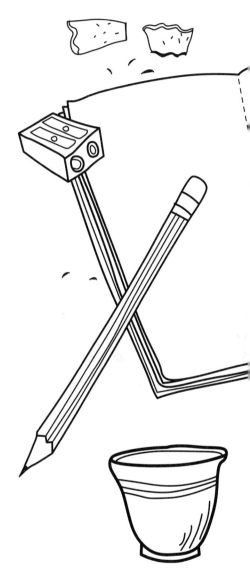

- Answer the phone, stating the name of your restaurant with necessary greetings.
  (Try to make a reservation for 8 p.m. the following Sunday.)

- Inform the caller that there will be a/will be no table available for that time.
  When there will be no table available, give the caller alternatives, such as another time.
  (Accept the time offered or ask for another time)

- Confirm the exact number of people will be present.
  (Be specific in giving information regarding the number of adults and young children)

- Ask for the caller for his or her name and the ways to contact him or her.
  (Give name and the phone number or other means for further contact.)

- Confirm the reservation by repeating the details. Thank the caller and tell him or her that you will be expecting his or her patronage.

　　預約在今天的社會中似乎已成為一種不可或缺的禮儀（etiquettes）；舉凡餐飲、美容、美髮、看醫生、見律師，若是先沒約時間就突然出現，很可能會招人白眼甚至於無法得到自己想要的服務。

　　當然，並不是每個地方都會要求事先預約；很多餐廳就會在顯眼的地方標示歡迎walk-ins（過路客），更會有人擺明 "No reservation accepted"（不接受預約）。一般而言，高檔高價位（high-end）的餐廳基於成本及服務品質考量，通常會堅持預約，但 eatery/mom-and-pop's place/diner（小本經營的餐廳）就不會太執著了。儘管如此，打電話查詢（making inquiries）時問清楚是否要訂位（Is a reservation necessary?）或商家是否接受訂位（Do you accept reservations?）總比到了現場才發現你前面有成千上百的人在等候要來得實際。

　　有時受邀出席正式宴會時，在邀請函（invitation）中往往會要求 "R.S.V.P."（repondez s'il vous plait, Please Respond，請答覆）也是一種預約的做法；出席人數的統計，座位的安排（seating arrangements）甚至於左鄰右舍之間是否相識或有過衝突都是必須適時答覆的原因！

Unit
2

Good evening, Mr./Mrs. ..., this way, please. 迎賓

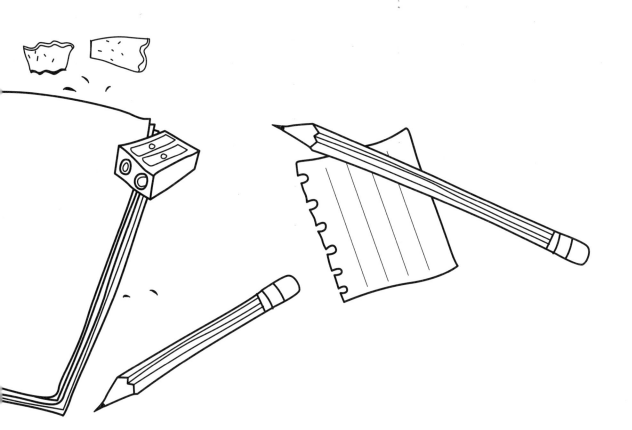

Read 閱讀

─────○─────

When greeting guests at the restaurants, it is important to bear in mind (牢記在心) that part of the receptionist's job is to make them feel as comfortable and welcome as possible. So, it would be a good idea for you to be familiar with some "small talks." (閒聊) Simple phrases like "How are you this evening?" and "How are you tonight?" are useful.

Sometimes, paying compliments (讚美) is another way to make someone feel welcome: "That's a lovely hat you have." or "I really like your dress."

Of course, asking questions will at other times do the trick (有效果): "Have you ever been to our restaurant before?" and "Where are you from?"

Don't forget the typical (典型) small talks topics like "Lovely weather we have today, isn't it?" and "Isn't the weather terrible?" A rule of thumb (基本規則): don't ask any personal questions, such as age, marital status (婚姻狀況) and religious (宗教) or political (政治) beliefs (信仰).

When seating (入座) a guest, you may find it helpful to offer the guest a choice rather than trying to seat them at a table that he or she does not like or want.

Seating small children can be a problem. Before the guest asks you for help, offer your services first. Suggest a baby chair (嬰兒椅) or a high chair (高腳椅) or a cushion (坐墊) whichever is available.

Single guests often prefer to be served over the counter (在 吧檯進食) in the coffee shop or bar rather than sit by themselves at a table.

In Chinese culture, the rules governing (決定影響) seating arrangements are complex; usually, the person with the highest position (職務) or status (地位), e.g. elderly person (長者) or the guest of honor (貴賓) should be seated facing the entrance (入門處) while host and/or hostess (男女 主人) are seated right next to him or her. Guests of less importance are situated (坐在) further away from the host depending on their importance.

However, the rules in the West are more flexible. The host usually sits at the shorter end of a rectangular table (長桌), the "head' of the table. As for the other people, there are many different ways of doing it. For example, people who know one another more are usually placed next to each other; also their social status and interests are sometimes taken into account when making seating arrangements with the most commonly held one be a man-woman-man-woman kind of arrangement.

Glossary: Words you can use 詞彙

─────○─────

A

actually	實際上
advisable	明智的
atmosphere/ambiance	氣氛／格調，周遭環境

B

buffet-style	自助餐式
by the way	順帶一提

C

catch of the day	本日／今日特餐（尤其是指海鮮食品）
check (out)	查看
chitchat	閒談，聊天說八卦
coat room/coat check	衣帽間
couldn't be better	再好也不過
cutlery	餐具（尤指刀叉湯匙）

D

daily special	本日／今日特餐
décor (decoration)	內部裝潢
drink	飲料

E

e.g. (= for example)	舉例說
expect	期待
extra	額外的，多出來的

F

follow	跟隨
furnishings	傢俱，陳設

H

Here we are!	到了
hold	保留
host/hostess	男女主人，男女接待

I

in a moment/momentarily	立即，立刻
it's about time	也該到時候了
in the meantime	同時

L

lectern	上置閱讀燈的講台；放置菜單的小櫃台
line/lineup	排隊

M

matire d'hotel (F)	領班
menu/menu board	菜單 (看板)
mind	介意，在意
mix-up/screw-up	混亂，弄錯的事

N

(paper) napkin	(紙) 餐

O

occasion	場合，盛會
offer	提供

P

parking coupon	停車卡 / 停車計費卡
parking lot/car park	停車場
patience	耐心
podium	(可移動式) 櫃台
prefer	情願，較喜歡

R

rapport	(相互) 關係
reception area	接待區

receptionist	接待員，領檯

S

small talk	閒談，寒暄
server	侍者

T

table setting	餐桌擺設
tableware	餐具 (盤子刀叉玻璃杯)
take out/takeaway food	外帶

U

under the name of	在…名下
uniform	制服

V

valet parking/self-parking	代客 / 自行停車
vegetarian menu	素食菜單
vegan	全素者 (不吃任何動物製品)
vegetarian	素食者

What to Say 情境對話

————○————

Situational Dialogue 1

🔘 2-1

R (Receptionist): Hello. Welcome to the Burger Heaven. How are we doing this evening?

G (Guest): Couldn't be better, thank you. How about yourself?

R Fine, thank you. Do you have a reservation for tonight?

G Yes, it's under the name of Smith. John Smith.

R Yes, I see it right here on the list: a party of four. Please follow me this way. Have you been to our restaurant before?

G No, actually, this is the first time. The atmosphere here is quite nice and the furnishings and décor, too.

R Well, thank you. Here is your table and your server will be with you in a moment. You might want to check out the daily specials on the menu board.

G I might just do that. Thanks very much.

Situational Dialogue 2

🔘 2-2

R Good evening. Welcome to the Red Lobster Restaurant. How are you this evening?

G Fine, thank you.

R Do you have a reservation for tonight?

G No, I'm afraid we don't.

R Well, there aren't any tables available at the moment, and the wait will be about 20 minutes. In the meantime, do you mind waiting a bit in the reception area or in the bar?

G No, that's perfectly alright with us. We could use a drink before dinner.

R Sure. I'll let you know when the first table becomes available. May I have your name?

G It's Smith, John smith.

Situational Dialogue 3　　　　　　　　　　　　　2-3

H (Hostess): Smith, party of four, your table is ready.

G That's us. It's about time.

H I'm really sorry for the wait. We are extremely busy today because of Father's Day. Please come this way.

G I guess I should make a reservation.

H It would advisable to make reservations on special occasions. Is this table OK?

G Not really. It's right next to the restroom.

H How about the table in the corner?

G That would be better. Thank you. Also, could you have our waiter bring us some paper napkins?

Situational Dialogue 4  2-4

H (Host): Good evening. Welcome to Seafood Paradise.

G Hello, a table for two, please.

H Yes, sir. Have you made a reservation?

G Yes, it's Smith. John Smith.

H Hmm, I can't seem to find your name on the list.

G There must be some mistake.

H When did you make the reservation?

G Just this afternoon around 1:30.

H I am terribly sorry about the mix-up. Your table will be ready momentarily.

G Thanks. By the way, do you have parking here?

H We offer valet parking, or, if you prefer, you can park yourself. There is a parking lot right next to the restaurant.

How to Say It 句型介紹

———○———

Followings are some useful expressions you can use when greeting and seating guests:

- Good morning/afternoon/evening. Welcome to _____ (name of the restaurant).

  How are you (doing) this morning/afternoon/evening?

  Hi, I'm _____ (name of the receptionist). Welcome to our restaurant.

- 常客寒暄問候

  Good morning/afternoon/evening, Mr. _____ (regular's/regular customer's name).

  Glad to see you again. Your table is already ready. We have been holding it for you.

- 確定是否有訂位

  Do you have a reservation?

  Have you made a reservation with us/our restaurant?

- 確定訂位名字

  What/Which name was the reservation made under?

  Under what/which name was the reservation booked?

- 訂位出問題

  I'm sorry, but I can't seem to find your name on the list.

  We don't seem to have a record of your reservation.

  May I ask when did you make the reservation?

- 帶路

  Would you come this way, please?

  Please step this way.

  Allow me to show you to your table.

- 耽誤

  I'm afraid the table you reserved is not ready yet.

  I'm afraid we let another guest sit at your table since you did not arrive at the reserved time.

- 等候

  I'm sorry, but there isn't any table (available) right now. There will be a wait of ___ minutes. May I have your name so that we can seat you as soon as we have a table.

- 分桌 / 和他人共桌

  The restaurant is full right now. Would you mind sitting separately.

  Would you mind sharing table with someone else?

- 通知就座

  Mr. _____ (name), party of ____ (number), your table is ready.

  Mr. _____ (name), we have a table for you now.

- 因錯誤而致歉

  I sincerely apologize for the mistake.

  I'm terribly sorry for the mix-up.

  Please accept our apologies for the error.

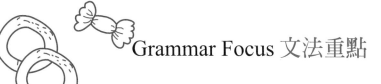

Grammar Focus 文法重點

———○———

本單元情境對話中有 "Do you mind waiting a bit in the reception area or in the bar?" 的用法。*Mind* 是動詞表示「介意」，其後通常和動名詞連用。

英文文法中有些動詞後一定要和動名詞連用：
acknowledge, admit, advise, advocate (主張鼓吹), anticipate, appreciate, avoid, complete, consider, contemplate (思量), defer (延緩), delay, deny, detest (厭惡), discuss, dislike, dread (害怕), ensure (保證), enjoy, escape, excuse, evade (躲避), facilitate (促成), fancy (想像), favor (擁護), forbid, finish, forgive, imagine, include, involve, keep, loathe (憎惡), mention, mind, miss (錯過), pardon (原諒), permit, postpone, practice, prevent, prohibit, propose, quit, recollect (回想), report, resent (討厭), resist, risk, save, suggest, tolerate, understand.

▶ Please pardon my disturbing you.
請原諒我打擾你。

▶ She said that she had always detested watching bullfight.
她說她總是討厭看鬥牛。

▶ He just missed being caught.
他才僥倖脫險。

有些片語中的 to，因為是當介系詞用，其後也必須加動名詞：
look forward to, with a view/an eye to , be accustomed to, be/get used to, have an objection to, pay attention to, in addition to, owing to, according to, thanks to, devote…to…

▶ The boy is looking forward to seeing his family.
男孩盼望看見自己的家人。

▶ Mary's parents have an objection to her quitting the school.
Mary 的父母親反對她放棄學業。

感官動詞如 hear, listen to, look at, see, smell 與如 catch, imagine, keep, leave, set, start 等動詞通常與下列句型連用：

S + V + O + V-ing

▶ I found John writing at his desk.
我發現 John 在他的書桌上寫東西。

▶ I caught the boy stealing flowers from my garden.
我抓到男孩從我花園中偷花。

下列片語通常也和動名詞連用, 但介係詞 in 通常可省略：

have difficulty/trouble/problem/a hard time/ fun/a good time + (in) + V-ing
waste time + (in) + V-ing
be busy + (in) + V-ing
lose (no) time + (in) + V-ing
no point + (in) + V-ing

▶ I wasted an hour studying the math only to find there will be no test for another week.
我花了一個小時讀數學後才發現要一個禮拜後才考試。

▶ There is no point arguing any further.
進一步的爭議沒用。

▶ They lost no time telling us the news.
他們一點時間也沒浪費就告訴我們這個消息。

Drills & Exercises

—— 練習 ——

A is a greeter at a restaurant and B is a guest who has not made a reservation. Use the following information and vocabulary you have learned in this unit to have a conversation.

Greeter:

- welcome the guest to the restaurant

- ask if the guest has made a reservation

- for guests without reservations, the wait will be 30 minutes

- tell the guest that due to a cancellation, he/she can be seated right away

- tell the guest to follow you; engage in some small talk to make him/her fell more comfortable

- tell the guest that all tables by the window have already been reserved

Guest:

- you have not made a reservation

- tell the greeter that you don't mind waiting; ask how long you will have to wait

- answer any small talk questions the greeter may ask you

- while the greeter is taking you to your seat, ask if you can sit by the window

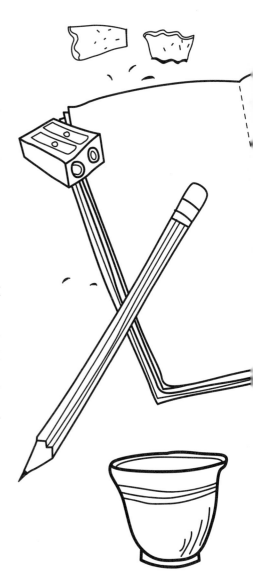

　　除了訂位時可能有特別要求外，另一個和位置相關的課題是餐具的擺設位置。

　　爲了營造優雅的氣氛，了解刀叉和餐盤的適當位置是件非常重要的事。通常，沙拉盤要放置在餐盤的上面，餐叉則放在餐盤的左側。沙拉叉應放置在餐叉的左側，而甜點叉則放在餐盤的上方。餐刀應放置在餐盤的右側，餐刀的刀鋒要朝向餐盤。餐刀的右側則放置舀湯的湯匙。麵包盤應放在餐盤的左上方，餐叉的上方，放在麵包盤上的奶油刀要水平放置，刀鋒朝下且指向左方。水杯和酒杯要放在餐刀和湯匙的上方，水杯靠近餐盤。茶杯與茶碟（供咖啡或茶使用）應放置在餐盤右上角，水杯和酒杯的左方。摺好的餐巾要放在叉子的左側，但有些餐廳會把餐巾放在玻璃杯內。

　　一般而言，先取用在外側的餐具，每道菜過後往內取用。將食物切成小塊時，應左手持餐叉，右手持餐刀；有些人認爲在進食時將叉子交到右手較禮貌（此時應將餐刀刀鋒朝內放在餐盤上），但也有人覺得左手持餐刀也無妨。喝東西時要將餐刀和餐叉置於餐盤上；一旦開始進食後，就不要把餐具置於餐桌上。如在用餐結束前必須離席，記得將餐具至於餐盤上。

　　開始進餐前把餐巾放在大腿上；切忌用餐巾擦拭餐具或擤鼻涕！用餐完畢後把餐巾摺起來放置在餐盤右邊；如果必須在進餐時離席，把餐巾摺好並放在桌上；不要把餐巾放在椅子上。

　　用餐結束後將刀叉依把手放在四點鐘方向，而刀鋒放在十點鐘方向的方式交叉置放在餐盤上，或是把餐具一起放置在餐盤中央。

　　以下的單元中，我們將會對進食時應注意的事項逐一說明。

Unit

3

Hi！I'm _____ and I will be your server tonight. 服務

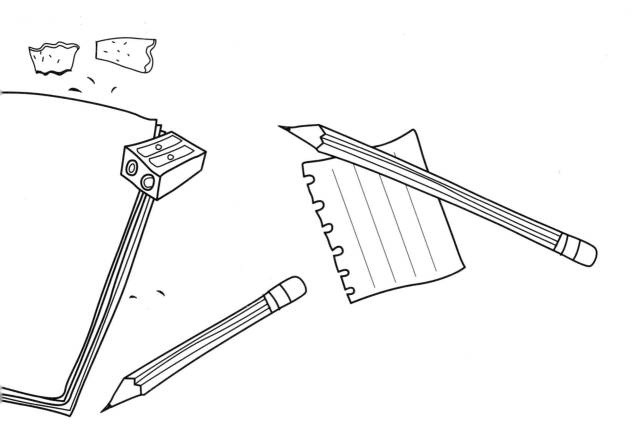

Read 閱讀

Serving food requires more than taking orders (接受點餐). Successful waiters and waitresses need to understand guidelines (準則) that will secure (確保) the establishment's customer base (客戶群) and increase their tips. Clear communication, product knowledge and anticipating (預期) customer needs are the keys to success. Polite and confident servers who respect their customers' patronage (惠顧) will find themselves successfully with respect to (在⋯方面) both monetary rewards (金錢獎賞) and job performance.

Introduce Yourself 自我介紹

Customers appreciate prompt (快速) service and should be approached (接近) within 30 seconds of being seated. Introductions should be made in a friendly (友善), relaxed (輕鬆) tone (語調) while looking customers in the eyes. Maintaining (保持) eye contact (目光接觸) indicates (顯示) undivided (全心全意) attention and portrays (顯現) confidence.

Know the Menu 了解菜單

Waiters and waitresses should know the menu and familiarize themselves with and daily specials (特餐). Customers

who ask for suggestions appreciate confident and quick replies (回覆) detailing (詳盡說明) other customers' preferences (喜愛). Product honesty (對產品質地的誠實) is refreshing (令人耳目一新的) and appreciated. It is also important to know dish ingredients (食材) and how they're prepared since customers may have dietary concerns (飲食的擔心).

Be Polite 禮儀

Good manners gain (獲得) respect and make an impression (造成印象). Customers respond better to those who respect and appreciate their patronage. Waiters and waitresses should never judge customers by pre-conceived (自以為是的) tipping (小費) notions (念頭) or stereotypes (刻板觀念) and should be polite to each individual they serve.

Refill Drinks 續杯

Great waiters and waitresses anticipate their customers' needs. Customers should never be parched (杯子乾了) during their meal. Water glasses should be constantly refilled, and coffee cups and teapots should be warmed or filled with permission (同意). Hot drinks should be poured away from the table to avoid accidents and should never be poured near a child. Customers appreciate servers who anticipate

their needs and will tip accordingly.

Frequent Tables 四處走動

Some customers require or demand more attention, while others may find constant attention irritating (困擾, 不適). Waiters and waitresses should use their intuition (直覺) to gauge (調整, 捉拿) their customer needs and frequent tables as required, remembering that it's important to visit tables once food has been served to determine customer satisfaction and respond to any condiment (調味料) needs.

Quality Check the Food Order 確定無誤

One of the most unheralded (無聞的; 不受重視的) waiter and waitress responsibilities is matching (一致) food orders to tables prior to (…之前) serving. Orders should be quality-checked prior to serving to ensure substitutions (替代品) or allergy (過敏) requests have been followed according to customer requests. When orders aren't correct, they should be sent back and the customer informed if there will be a brief delay (短暫的耽擱). When food arrives at a table, customers expect to eat; the disappointment that occurs if an incorrect meal is delivered is worse than the wait for the correct order.

Asses Bad Tips 評估小費

Bad tips should be assessed by servers as an opportunity to improve their service, since they're usually the result of something customers perceived (認 為) as being substandard (不合標準). Some customers leave small tips because they don't understand the tipping scale (標準) or don't have the necessary funds (錢), so all tips should be appreciated and customers wished a good evening.

Glossary: Words you can use 詞彙

A

accordingly	因此，所以
a la carte	單點
allergic to	對…過敏
anticipate	期待，期盼
appreciate	感激，激賞
approach	趨近，接近
assess	評估
aware	知道，察覺

B

bacon bits	碎鹹肉 (培根)

C

chef	廚師，主廚
clam chowder	蛤蜊巧達濃湯
concern (n.)	關心，關切，憂慮
condiment	調味料，佐料 (如鹽、胡椒等)

D

demand	要求
dressing	沙拉醬
dietary	飲食的

E

early-bird special	提早進食的優惠
establishment	公私立設施，機構，商店，公司
familiarize	熟悉

F

folk	大伙人
frequent (v.)	常去，常在，常出入
fund	金錢，資金
French onion soup	法式洋蔥湯

G

guideline	準則

I

in a row	連續
ingredient	食材，成分
in season	當季
intuition	直覺
irritating	惱人的，令人憤怒的

J

judge	打量，評價

M

manners	禮儀，禮節
mashed potato	薯泥
match	配合，與…一致
monetary	金錢的

N

notion	觀念，想法

P

pass	放棄
parched	口乾舌燥的
patronage	光臨，惠顧
perceive	感覺，感受
portion	份量
portray	描繪
pour	倒 (酒飲料咖啡茶)
pre-conceived	預想的，先入為主的
preference	偏愛；選擇
prior to...	之前

Q

quality-check	品質檢驗

R

recommend	推薦
roast	烤
refill (v.)	添加
refreshing	令人爽快的
region	區域
relaxed	輕鬆的，不拘形式的
reply (n.)	回答，回覆
respond	回應
responsibility	職責，工作職掌
reward	獎賞，報酬

S

scale	(收費)等級
serving	份量
side dish	配菜
sole	比目魚，碟魚
sour cream	酸奶油
specialty	本行，專長
stereotype	陳腔濫調，刻板印象
substitution	替代物
substandard	次級，次等
surf 'n turf	海陸大餐

T

table d'hote	套餐
tips (To Insure Prompt Service)	小費

U

undivided	全神貫注的
unheralded	未告知的；不為人所知的

What to Say 情境對話

―――○―――

Situational Dialogue 1

🔊 3-1

W (Waiter): Hi! I am John, and I will be your server tonight. How are you folks doing this evening?

C (Customer): Pretty good. How about yourself?

W Good. Care for something to drink from the bar while you're looking at the menu?

G We're good, thank you. Some water will be nice, though.

W No problem. Are you ready to order, or do you need more time?

G Can we have more time to look over the menu? It's been a while since we last ate here.

W Sure. I'll be back shortly with your bread sticks and some water.

G That'll be great.

Situational Dialogue 2

🔊 3-2

W May I take your order now?

G Yes. But before that, what's today's special? I can't seem to find it on the menu board.

W Oh, I'm sorry. For $ 16.95, you can have the seafood platter with your choice of vegetables on the side, and for $ 19.95, you can have the whole barbequed ribs or half if the serving is too big for you for just $ 10.95.

G Hmmm. What about soups? What's the Soup of the Day?

W It's New England clam chowder. Or French onion soup if you prefer.

G Well, I am allergic to seafood, so I'll pass on the seafood platter. The barbequed ribs sounds good to me. Ma'am would you recommend that?

W With all my heart, sir. As a matter of fact, our barbequed ribs have been listed as one of the top ten served in this region three years in a row.

G That's something I'll have to try.

Situational Dialogue 3   3-3

W (Waitress): Would you like to have table d'hote, or a la carte?

G (Customer): I can't decide.

W Today's special is beef steak with wild mushrooms. It is always a favorite with our customers. And our specialty is roast leg of lamb.

G No, I'm not that hungry. What else do you recommend?

W Perhaps you'd like some sole?

G That would be fine.

W Would you like a salad with it, sir?

G Yes, a mixed salad, please. What kind of dressing do you have?

W We have ranch, Thousand Island, French and Italian.

G French, please. Also, please make sure that the dressing is on the side.

Situational Dialogue 4

W Have you decided what to order, ma'am?

G Almost. What does the surf 'n turf come with?

W The meal comes with your choice of two kinds of vegetables.

G Good, I'll have the surf 'n turf.

W Excellent choice. Would you like to order any side dishes? Baked potato, mashed potatoes, or French fries, maybe?

G I think I'll have a baked potato.

W Sure. Would you care for sour cream and bacon bits with your potato?

G Yes, thank you. I might want to have some dessert later.

W I'll bring you a dessert menu.

How to Say It 句型介紹

———○———

Followings are some useful expressions you can use before serving guests and ordering meals:

- Here is the menu/wine list/dessert menu, sir/ma'am. The waiter will be here to take your order.

- 詢問是否可以開始點菜：

  Excuse me, sir/ma'am. May I take your order now?

  Are you ready to order, sir/ma'am?

  Are you ready to order or you need another minute?

- 詢問客人的飲食禁忌，喜好或特殊需要：

  We have both buffet-style dinner and a la carte dishes, which you prefer?

  If there anything you can't eat?

  Are you allergic to any particular food?

  Are you on a special diet?

  We serve .... (Cantonese, Sichuan, Shanghai, Beijing/ Chinese, American, European) cuisines, which cuisine would you prefer?

  Would you like large/small portions/servings?

- 推薦菜品：

  Today's special/The Early Bird special is...

  The .... is excellent/terrific and I highly recommend it.

  We have a wide range/selection of .... (vegetarian,...) dishes to choose from.

  May I suggest...? It's our house specialty.

  The ... is in season now. Would you like to try it?

  Have you tried ....? It's our chef's specialty.

  The set course is as delicious but much cheaper, and it won't cost you much time if you're in a hurry.

- 沒有客人需要的食物：

... is out of the season right now. How about ...?

I'm sorry, there is no ... today.

I'm afraid ... is not on our menu, but I'll check with our chef and see if it is available.

I'm afraid ... is sold out.

I'm afraid ... is not available right now. Would you like to try ...? It's also very tasty.

Note

Grammar Focus 文法重點

———— ○ ————

"We have *both* Chinese and American cuisines served in our restaurant."

"You can have the choice of *either* baked *or* mashed potato."

"*Neither* of the dishes you mentioned is available now because they are out of the season."

"*Not all* the dishes on the menu are available. Check with your waiter/waitress before order."

上述四個句子中分別用到 "*both*," "*either... or ...*," "*neither*," 和 "*not all*."

這四種表達都屬於不定代名詞，其用法分述如下：

兩者皆有時用 *both*，兩者皆無時用 *neither*，兩者選一時用 *either*，兩者裡一有一無（部份否定）時用 *not both*；

三者皆有時用 *all*，三者皆無食用 *none*，三者選一時用 *any*，三者裡有的有有的無（部份否定）時用 not all。

比較：

Not both of the servers are diligent.

Neither of the waiters is diligent.

Not all of the dishes were tasty.

Some of the dishes are tasty, but some aren't.

Both 只能用於複數可數名詞且指兩個，若當主詞用時其後接複數形動詞；

All 代表可數名詞時其後接複數形動詞，代表不可數名詞時其後接單數形動詞。

Both of them are old enough to drink.

All of them are to come to the party tomorrow.

All of his money was spent on food.

—— 練習 ——

Put the sentences below in order by numbering them from 1 to 8.

- ___ G: What's Today's Special?

- ___ H: I believe it's out of the season. But I'll double-check with the chef to make sure.

- ___ H: Are you ready to order, or you need more time?

- ___ G: Can I have sole instead? Do you serve sole in your restaurant?

- ___ H: We have grilled trout for 16.95 and roast leg of lamb baked to perfection for 19.95, both of them come with your choice of vegetables.

- ___ H: Excellent choice if I may say so. How about side dishes?

- ___ G: In that case, my lady friend will have the lamb and I'll have the grilled trout. We both will have the mixed salad with Italian dressing on the side.

- ___ G: No, we'll pass. We'd like to save some room for the dessert.

- double-check: 再確定
- grill: 烤 (肉)；大塊烘烤
- trout: 鱒魚
- roast: 烤 (魚)；燒炙
- leg of lamb: 羊腿
- in that case: 那麼
- pass: 放棄
- room: (肚子) 空間

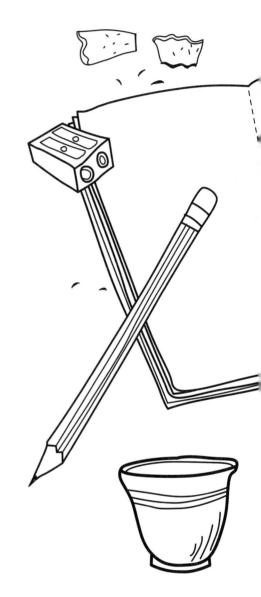

在進餐時，儘管還沒拿到餐點的人會堅持已拿到的人先用餐，但是通常要等大家的餐點都到了才開始用餐，這樣才是有禮貌的表現。如果是正式晚宴，賓客該等主人開始用餐後才開動。

打嗝（to burp）或在進食時發出聲響（to slurp）或張大嘴巴咀嚼或在嘴裡還有食物時開口說話（to chew or speak when the mouth is full）等都會被視爲沒有禮貌。把食物從嘴裡吐出來也件無禮的行爲；如果吃到了不想吃的食物，記得：用什麼方式送進嘴裡就用什麼方式取出，如果用的是叉子，就用叉子把食物拿出來。但用手把魚刺或骨頭拿出嘴巴是可以被接受的作法。有些特定食物如漢堡、三明治、披薩、雞翅、肋條、玉米等可以用手拿來吃，甚至於在進食後還可以用舔手指來表示味美及意猶未盡（Yummy！）

如果你喜歡某道菜餚，也想多吃一點甚至再來一份（another/the second serving），雖然沒有必要將盤中已有的食物吃個精光，但也別留下太多的剩菜（leftover）。如果灑了（spilt）飲料在桌上或餐具掉到桌下，最好要求服務生代勞清理；若在某人家中，則該自行清理或自行撿起來並要求一副乾淨的餐具。不要爲了拿離你很遠的食物而將身體靠在他人身上；有禮貌地要求他人將食物傳給你。把菜遞給下一位時，正確的方向是往右手邊傳遞；如果你不喜歡所傳遞過來的食物，直接遞給下一位即可。

Unit

4

Something from the bar, perhaps?
(Beverages) 飲料

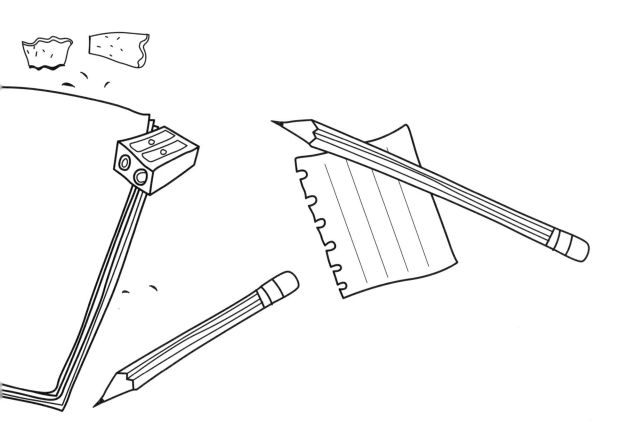

Read 閱讀

An alcoholic beverage (酒類飲品) is a drink containing ethanol (乙醇), commonly known as alcohol. Alcoholic beverages are divided into three categories: beers, wines, and spirits (烈酒). The production and consumption (消耗使用) of alcohol occurs in most cultures of the world, and are often an important part of social events in these cultures.

Beer is one of the world's oldest and most widely consumed alcoholic beverages, and the third most popular drink overall after water and tea. Wine is produced from grapes, and from fruits such as plums (李子), cherries, or apples. Spirits are alcoholic beverages that have the highest alcohol content (高酒精濃度) of all; for the most common beverages such as whisky and vodka, the alcohol content is around 40%.

People drink alcoholic beverages for various reasons:
- They are part of people's standard diet (飲食)
- They are drunk for medical reasons
- For their relaxant (緩和) effects
- For their euphoric (心情愉快) effects
- For recreational (消遣 , 娛樂) purposes

● For artistic inspiration (藝術感染力)

However, not all people share the same ideas when it comes to alcohol:

In India, drinking alcohol in public is prohibited (禁止); in Japan, alcoholic beverages can be sold from vending machines (自動販賣機) and public drunkenness (公共醉酒) is not viewed as illegal (非法); in Denmark, it is generally legal to drink alcoholic beverages in the streets, but the consumption of alcohol in outdoor areas except those immediately (緊鄰地) outside the bar/pub will be illegal. Drinking alcohol in public places, such as streets and parks, is against the law in most of the United States; whereas in the United Kingdom, drinking in public places is not banned (禁止) by national laws, but some cities and towns have by-laws (章程, 附則) that prohibit possessions (持有) of an open container (容器) of alcohol in public place.

A soft drink (also called soda 汽水 , pop 含氣飲料 , coke, soda pop, fizzy drink 碳酸飲料 , tonic 奎寧水 , seltzer 碳酸水 , mineral 礦泉水 , sprinkling water 氣泡水 or carbonated beverage 含二氧化碳的飲料) is a beverage that typically contains water, a sweetener (糖精), and a flavoring agent (香料劑). Soft drinks may also contain caffeine (咖

啡因), colorings (色素), preservatives (防腐劑) and other ingredients. Widely sold soft drink flavors (味道) are cola, cherry, lemon-lime (萊姆), root beer (沙士), orange, grape, vanilla, ginger, ale (麥芽), fruit punch (果汁噴趣 , 水果雞尾酒), and sparkling lemonade (汽泡檸檬汁). Soft drinks may be served chilled or at room temperature; they are rarely heated.

Though it may sound as innocent as the word "soft" suggests, drinking too much soft drinks can still result in some health problems; obesity (肥 胖) and weight-related diseases, bone loss (骨質流失) and dental decay (蛀牙) just to name a few. Like alcoholic beverages which has been scientifically proved that has a very strong connection with heart disease, dementia (失智症), cancer, diabetes (糖尿病), stroke (中風), and obesity, "moderation" (適量節制) is the key in consuming both.

Other than alcoholic and soft beverages, some people prefer to drink water. People believe that drinking water will help you clear out toxins (毒素), that it will give better and healthier skin, and that it will help you lose weight. Though no solid scientific evidences have suggested that all the aforementioned (上述的) benefits from drinking water are

true, it is still advisable to drink water when one feels needed since it has no calories (卡路里，熱量) and it does have some effects on skin. But, how do you know if you're drinking enough water? An easy way to judge: if you are not thirsty, your fluid intake is likely "just right."

Glossary: Words you can use 詞彙

A

aftertaste	餘味
(brown/pale) ale	（深色／淺色的）麥芽啤酒
aroma	香味

B

barista	煮咖啡師傅
bartender	酒保，調酒師
beer on tap	生啤酒
(drought/draft) beer	散裝啤酒
bitter	有苦味的
bottled	瓶裝的
bouquet	酒香味
brand	品牌
breathe	讓氣味散發
buy one and get one free	買一送一

C

canned	罐裝的
carbonated	含二氧化碳的
chaser	飲用烈酒後的飲料如水或啤酒
chilled	冷凍
cocktail	雞尾酒
competent	稱職的，合格的

cork	軟木塞
corked	有軟木塞味
cork screw	螺絲開瓶起子

D

dark beer	黑啤酒
delicate	清淡可口的
designated driver	指定駕駛
domestic	本地／國的
double	雙份的（酒精量）
dry	不甜的，無果味的

E

earthy	有土味的

F

fiery	激烈的，燒喉的
finer	美好的
fizzy	起泡的
flavor	風味
foam	奶泡
full-bodied	香醇濃郁的

G

gents	男士

H

happy hour	歡樂時間（指酒吧的減價時段）
hit the road	上路
house wine	招牌（平價）酒；若為高價酒則可說成 premium wine

I

ice bucket	冰桶
imported	進口的
indulge	放縱
intake	攝取

J

juice	果汁

L

last call	酒吧打烊前的最後點酒的機會
Last one for the road, drink coffee!	勸戒飲酒者在上路前喝杯咖啡保持清醒
lager	微淡多泡的啤酒

layer	層
liquor	酒
lounge	休息室

M

milder	較溫和 / 淡的
minors	未成年者
mug	馬克杯

N

night-cap	睡前酒

O

oblige	配合；遵守
on the rocks	加冰塊
on the wagon	戒酒

P

pretzel	椒鹽脆餅
proof	酒精濃度
put...on tab	記帳

R

reminder	提醒
retire	告退，就寢
rice wine	米酒
rich	味濃的
rosseta	（咖啡的）拉花
round	一回，一巡

S

Sake	清酒
single/double	調酒中一份或兩份基酒
signature	拿手的，具代表性的
sip	啜
sommelier	酒侍，斟酒的侍應生
somewnat	有些
straight (up)	不加任何東西的純酒

T

tempt	誘惑

V

virgin	純的，不加酒精的

W

well balanced	平順的
well drinks	比較普通但未必廉價的基酒所調製的酒
(house/premium) wine	（招牌／高檔）葡萄酒

What to Say 情境對話

———○———

Situational Dialogue 1　　　　　　　　　　　　　　🔘 4-1

S (Server): Hi, I am John and I'll be your server this evening. Would you care for something from the bar before your meal?

G (Guest): That sounds like a good idea; I can sure use a beer. What kind of beer on tap you have?

S I'm sorry but we don't carry draft beer at our restaurant; however, we have excellent imported bottled ales and lagers.

G I prefer dark beer. What kinds of ales do you have?

S I recommend the German beers, Belgian beers are a good choice as well; they are high in alcoholic content and taste somewhat bitter.

G I'll take a German beer; I'm not driving anyway. My husband is the designated driver for the night.

Situational Dialogue 2　　　　　　　　　　　　　　🔘 4-2

S (Sommelier): Can I tempt you with our wine list, sir? We have a wide selection of reds and whites to choose from.

G (Guest): What's your house wine?

S We have French Bordeaux and California Cabernet and both of them are full-bodied wines with aroma and taste flavorful and well balanced. As for the premium wines, we have French Chablis, Riesling and Chardonnay; we also have Italian Merlot and Swiss Pinot Noir for your pleasure.

G Actually, I am not that big a fan of wine; I am just trying to indulge myself once in a while.

S You really don't need to be an expert to enjoy something finer. And our house wines are sold by the glass just in case they do not meet your satisfaction.

G In that case, we'll have two glasses of your fine French Chardonnay.

Situational Dialogue 3   4-3

S (Server): Can I get you anything to drink from the bar?

G (Guest): No thank you, I am on the wagon. What kind of non-alcoholic drinks do you have?

S Well, our award-winning barista makes excellent Caramel Macchiato and Café Latte with a layer of foam and rosseta. Other than those, we also offer a variety of freshly squeezed juices and mineral waters. Of course soft drinks like Coke, Pepsi or Sprite are available as well.

G It sounds wonderful. I think I'll have your signature Caramel Macchiato. And my daughter will have some juice.

S Sure. Do you want the drinks served with your desserts? Or, you want them now?

G We'd like to have them now.

S I'll be right back with your drinks and your order.

Situational Dialogue 4

B (Bartender): What can I get your gents?

G (Guest): Do you have Happy Hour at this restaurant?

B Yes, we do. It's from 5 p.m. to 7 p.m. During these hours, you can buy one drink and get one free.

G That's something we'll have to take advantage of. What do you think, guys? Should we order a round of drinks?

B You want me bring your free drinks at the same time or after you've finished with your first round?

G Afterwards will be better.

B Just a reminder, the last call is 11:30 p.m.

B That's a greyhound, a Jonnie Walker Black on the rocks and another one straight up with a beer chaser, a virgin bloody Mary, and two glasses of house white. Would you like to pay for your drinks now or should I put it on your tab?

G Putting it on my tab will be fine, thanks. And can you make that Jonnie Walker on the rocks a double?

B Sure. I will be right back with your drinks along with some peanuts and pretzels.

How to Say It 句型介紹

───── ○ ─────

Followings are some useful expressions you can use when ordering beverages:

- Would you like to order some wine with your meal?
  And what drink would you like with your ___ (餐點食物)?

- 推薦飲品
  Would you like to try our ___ (酒品)?
  I think ___ (酒名) would go very well with your ___ (食物，餐點).
  We have chilled and heated Sake. Which one would you like?
  Would you care for something stronger/milder?
  We have ___ (酒名) if you prefer something stronger/milder.
  We serve ___, ____, ____ (酒名) and so on. What would you like?
  How would you like ___ (酒名), straight up or on the rocks?

- 詢問需要
  With or without ice, sir/ma'am?
  Straight up, sir/ma'am?
  Just say "when," sir/ma'am. (請告訴我何時停)
  The same again, sir/ma'am?
  Another round, perhaps?
  A night-cap before retiring, sir/ma'am?
  Last one before you hit the road, sir/ma'am?

- 拒絕客人要求
  I'm sorry but no minors are allowed in the bar.
  The law specifically request that no one under the age of 18 is allowed in this area.
  The drink might not be suitable for children since it has alcohol in it.
  I'd like to oblige but I have my difficulty.
  Last one for the road, how about some coffee?

Grammar Focus 文法重點

——○——

英文中有些用法，意思看似相同但實際上卻有些不同的意義或規定：

would like to + (to + V 原形)

feel like + V-ing

▶ I would like to eat out tonight.
今晚我想到外面吃飯。

▶ I don't feel like going out tonight.
今晚我不想外出。

▶ He is gone.
他走了。（表示狀態）

▶ He has gone.
他已走了。（表示動作完成）

▶ He is nothing but a liar.
他除了是騙子外什麼都不是。

▶ He is anything but a liar.
他什麼都是就是不是騙子。

▶ We can do nothing to do but wait.
除了等以外我們什麼事都不能做。

▶ He does nothing but play all day.
他整日除了玩以外什麼事都不做。

▶ This is the same watch that I have lost.
這正是我遺失的手錶。

▶ This is the same watch as I have lost.
這手錶和我遺失的一樣。

——— 75 ———

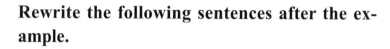

Drills & Exercises

——— 練習 ———

Rewrite the following sentences after the example.

Example: Look at the label on the wine bottle. (take)
Take a look at the label on the wine bottle.

1. They walked together. (take)

2. Our manager will visit France this summer. (pay)

3. Ann rested after a ten-mile walk. (take)

4. I talked with her yesterday afternoon. (have)

5. May I look at it? (take)

Select the correct form in the parentheses in the following sentences:

1. Of the four coats, I like the black one (better/best).

2. Jack is the (compententest/most competent) waiter we have ever known.

3. Jane's speed is (fastest/the fastest) than any other waitress at the restaurant.

4. Does Sean feel (better/weller) today than he was yesterday?

5. This onion soup tastes very (well/good)

6. The recipe calls for (many/much) sugar than usual when baking the sponge cake.

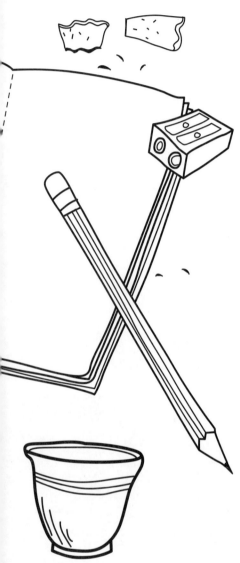

7. The men servants felt (worse/worst) than the women servants after losing the contest.

8. The price at restaurant A is much cheaper than (that/those) at restaurant B.

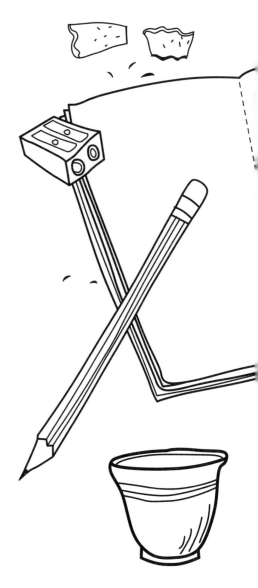

　　拿酒杯的正確的方式是拿著它的杯腳；如果你把手放在杯碗（the 'bowl' part of a glass），酒的溫度會因為手的握持而急速上升，因而改變酒的風味。杯碗的大小則會因為喝白酒或紅酒甚至於甜酒泡沫酒香檳時所用的玻璃杯不同而有異。

　　記得：喝任何飲料時，喝出聲音或喝完後舔舐嘴唇都會被視為不禮貌。喝飲料時，牛飲（to drink like a fish; gulp down）不是件值得鼓勵的事。淺酌（to sip）不僅看起來文明多了，而且能真正的嘗出飲品的風味。

　　如果你不喝酒，只需要告訴服務生你不需要酒即可，或在服務生靠近斟酒時輕輕將手放在玻璃杯上也可以。添加飲食時，侍應生通常會說 "Just say when." 這句話的意思是「夠了就說」。這個用法又再次證明：英文翻譯絕不只是把每個字詞的意思弄懂就夠了！

　　因酒後駕車（DUI, to drive under the influence of alcohol; intoxicated）而導致致命的事件時有所聞；不僅害己同時也害人！指定駕駛（designated driver）這個觀念也因此而應運而生。在社交聚會或活動（social gathering/event/function）中，一定有一人滴酒不沾，而這人的工作就是在活動結束後，將每個人都平安送回家。有人會因為不喝酒但愛和朋友混在一起（to hang out with friends）而擔任指定駕駛；其他時候則是大家輪流（to take turns）來擔任這個工作；不論是何種狀況，快快樂樂出門，平平安安回家才是休閒應酬時的最高指導原則（guideline）！

Unit
5

Something sure smells good！(Breakfast)
Food orders 早餐

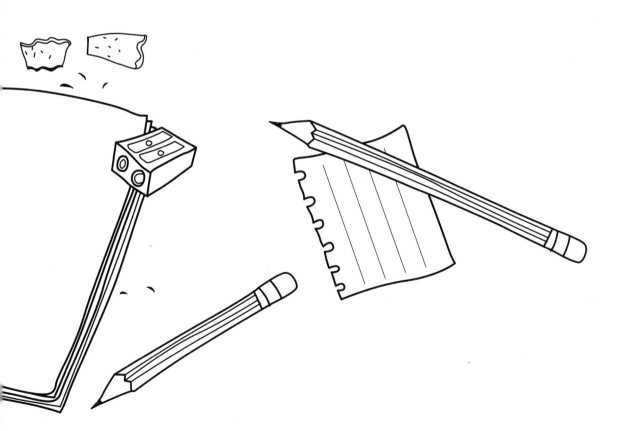

The word breakfast is a compound (複合字) of "break" and "fast (禁食)," referring to the conclusion of fasting (禁食, 齋戒) since the previous day's last meal. Nutrition (營養) experts have referred to breakfast as the most important meal of the day, citing (引用) studies (研究) that find that people who skip (省略) breakfast are disproportionally (一面倒) likely to have problems with concentration (集中注意力), metabolism (新陳代謝), and weight.

A good breakfast makes an excellent start of the day. It provides us with a sufficient portion (部分：一份餐點) of nutrients (營養品), energy and positive (正面, 積極) emotions. Some of us prefer a bowl of cereal (穀類) with low-fat milk for breakfast, some prefer a sandwich with a cup of tea or coffee, some opt for (選擇) traditional, for the westerners, omelet (燕 麥) or 2 eggs or steamed rice and/or porridge/congee (稀飯) with preserved/pickled vegetable (醬菜) for Asians, some enjoy having a little bit of yogurt (優 酪 乳) with fruits, and some can choose protein (蛋白質) cocktail or a smoothie (養生凍飲). Unfortunately, sometimes a good breakfast cannot find way to our tables in the morning, so we leave home and start our day with having a meal.

The dangers of skipping breakfast include slowed down metabolism (新陳代謝) and calorie burning, increased blood pressure, tiresome and inability to focus, higher risks of psychological disorders (心理失調) and cardiovascular diseases (心臟疾病) and many other negative factors. The followings are some facts you should know about breakfast:

- The idea that skipping breakfast can help us reduce our daily calorie consumption is incorrect. Studies have shown that skipping breakfast leads to increased hunger and increased calorie consumption (消耗) later the day.

- Skipping breakfast causes slowed down metabolism and other processes in the body, leading to less calorie burning, less fat loss and increased risks of weight gain. 49% of modern adults admit that they have to struggle to get through the day in case if they skipped breakfast in the morning.

- The best and the healthiest breakfast should include about 20 g proteins, plenty of dietary fiber and less than 5 g fats. Also, it should have the main vitamins and minerals, including vitamin B complex (維他命 B 群), vitamin C and A (維他命 C & A), potassium (鉀), calcium (鈣), manganese (錳), zinc (鋅), iron, and phosphorus (磷).

- Do not forget to measure (測量) your breakfast portions and avoid overeating. Consuming too much of foods for breakfast (especially too sweet or too fatty foods) can cause heaviness (鬱 悶) in the stomach, shortness

of breath (氣上不來), metabolic malfunctioning (失能), psychological and emotional distress (苦惱, 憂傷), and other negative factors.

- According to the findings of the scientists, breakfast is a great way to avoid wasting foods and save the money. It is estimated that by having breakfast on a daily basis we can avoid about $2 billion worth waste, mainly yogurt and bread, which is over 1 million tons of food.

Remember: Breakfast like a king, lunch like a prince, and dinner like a pauper (乞丐) !

Glossary: Words you can use 詞彙

---○---

A

additives	添加物
American breakfast	美式早餐 (包含蛋、吐司、培根 / 火腿肉 / 鹹肉 / 香腸、咖啡 / 茶、果汁)
appetite	胃口

B

bacon	煙燻豬肉，培根
baked bean	加紅糖 (brown sugar) 和肥豬肉 (bacon/pork belly) 煮熬的黃豆
bagel	貝果，硬麵包圈
(soft/hard) boiled egg	(蛋黃未熟 / 蛋黃全熟) 水煮蛋
Bon appetite (F.)	祝胃口大開
buffet	自助餐式
buckwheat	蕎麥
steamed stuffed bun	包子

C

chunk potato/potato chunk	炒的塊狀馬鈴薯
cinnamon roll	肉桂捲
(cold/hot) cereal	(冷 / 熱) 穀類製品食物，麥片
(regular/decaffeinated/flavored) coffee	(普通 / 低咖啡因 / 調味) 咖啡
congee	稀飯，粥

continental breakfast	歐式 / 大陸早餐 (包含餐包 / 牛角麵包 / 糕餅、水果、咖啡 / 茶 / 果汁)
corn beef (hash)	醃鹹牛肉 (泥)
cornflake	玉米片
crack course	速成班
cream	乳脂，奶精
crispy	脆的
croissant	牛角麵包

D

dim sum	(廣式) 點心
dipped	沾

E

egg Benedict	班尼迪克蛋 (以首創者命名的早餐蛋)
(full) English breakfast	(全) 英式早餐 (包含煎 / 炒 / 煮蛋、鹹肉香腸、菇類、布丁、吐司、咖啡 / 茶)

F

fat	脂肪
fiber	纖維

French toast	法式吐司
fried bread stick/deep-fried twisted dough stick	油條
fried egg (over-hard)	煎蛋 (蛋黃全熟)
fried egg (over-easy)	煎蛋 (蛋黃未熟)

G

granola	燕麥捲 / 棍
granulated sugar	砂糖

H

ham	火腿
hash browns	薯餅
honey	蜂蜜

I

in store for	替…準備著

J

jam/jelly	(有 / 無果肉的) 果醬

M

made-to-order	現做
marmalade	含果粒的果醬

(whole/low-fat/non-fat or skim) milk	(全脂 / 低脂 / 無脂) 牛奶
mix/mixture	混合物
muffin	英式鬆餅

N

nectar	花蜜

O

oatmeal/porridge	燕麥 / 麥片粥
omelet	蛋捲

P

pancake	薄鬆餅
(Danish) pastry	加有果醬或水果的糕餅
poached egg	水煮荷包蛋
powdered sugar	糖粉
preserved/pickled vegetables	醬菜
preservatives	防腐劑
protein	蛋白質

R

raisin (bran)	葡萄乾 (麥片)
raspberry	覆盆子

refill	續杯
rich	濃郁
runny	稀的

S

salty duck egg	鹹蛋
sausage	香 / 臘腸
savory	鹹的
scrambled egg	炒蛋
seasonal	當季的
stack	(一)疊
steamed/fried dumpling	蒸 / 煎餃
stick to	堅持
strip	條 (如培根)
sweet/salty soybean milk	甜 / 鹹豆漿
(maple) syrup	(楓) 糖漿

T

| (white/whole-wheat/rye) toast | (白 / 全麥 / 裸麥) 吐司 |

W

| whipped | 打的 (蛋 / 奶油) |

What to Say 情境對話

───○───

Situational Dialogue 1

 5-1

G (Guest): Excuse me, I realize it might be too late, but are you still serving breakfast?

W (Waitress): Yes, we are. Actually, we are open for breakfast 24/7, round the clock. Here is the breakfast menu.

G Great, thanks. Let's see, the American breakfast looks good. I think I'll have that.

W No problem. How would you like your eggs?

G Scrambled, please. But make sure they aren't runny.

W Sure. And would you care for some bacon, ham or sausage?

G Bacon sounds good, extra crispy, please. By the way, how about some white toast, not whole wheat.

W Are you sure you don't want to try our rye and whole-wheat bread?

G I'll stick to the white. Thanks anyway, though.

Situational Dialogue 2

 5-2

G Excuse me, miss. What's French toast?

W It's two slices of bread dipped in an egg mixture, pan-fried, in butter with cinnamon, and served with syrup.

G That's kind of rich, isn't it? Also, I don't think I'm that hungry.

W Then, how about the Continental breakfast? It has croissants, Danishes, seasonal fresh fruit, coffee and freshly-squeezed orange juice.

G That's much better. I think I'll have that. What about refills for the coffee?

W The first refill is free and, after that, it will be $.50 for additional ones.

G I think one refill is quite enough, caffeine you know.

W We also have decaffeinated coffee if you like. It's almost the same in flavor as the regular one.

G Regular coffee will be all right.

Situational Dialogue 3   🔅 5-3

W (Waiter): Are you here for the breakfast buffet, or would you like to order something from the menu?

G I don't really have that big an appetite. I think I'll just have some pancakes. How many are there in a stack?

W Three. And you can have your choice of ham, bacon or sausage.

G I will pass on the meat. Does it come with syrup?

W Yes, it does. Would you also like powdered sugar on top of it as well?

G That would be nice. Some fruit on the side would be even better.

W We have blueberries, strawberries and raspberries.

G The strawberries, please. And a cup of coffee if you can.

Situational Dialogue 4

G1 Well, as they say, "When in Rome do as the Romans do;" How about some Chinese breakfast?

G2 That'll be interesting to find what they have in store for us on the menu.

G1 Oh, waiter. How about a crash course on Chinese breakfasts?

W Chinese breakfast varies from region to region. You can have Dim Sums, along with some tea, which is very popular in Chinatowns around the world.

G2 What is Dim Sum?

W They are little snacks, usually steamed, deep fried, or boiled, and the variety is enormous.

G1 What are the other options?

W You can have delicious noodles if you are into that, or steamed stuffed bun or deep-fried twisted stick and sweet or salty soybean milk. Or, you can have congee served with salty duck egg and pickled vegetables if you like rice for breakfast.

G2 I think we'll try the Dim Sum today and save the rest for another time.

How to Say It 句型介紹

———○———

Followings are some useful expressions you can use when ordering breakfast:

- 詢問

  Could you tell me what ... (English breakfast/American breakfast) is?

  How many are there ... (in a stack/ in the basket)?

  Can I have ... instead?

  Can I have low-fat milk instead for my coffee?

- 查詢或提供選擇

  Would you like to...?

  Would you prefer... to...?

  How about some... for a change?

- 詢問做法

  How would you like ... (eggs) done?

  Would you like to have ... (whipped cream/powdered sugar) on the top/side?

  How about (some)... (coffee/tea/water)?

  What kind of ... (bread/fruit)would you prefer/do you want?

- 選擇

  I would like it ... (extra crispy/over-easy/sunny-side up/...)

  I would like ... (a refill for my coffee/ a second serving of the same thing).

  How about ... (a refill)?

- 解釋說明

  ... is like ... except that...

  Congee is like porridge except that it's more watery and is made of rice.

  ... is served with your choice of...

  The French toast is served with your choice of bacon, ham and sausages.

- 同意或嘉許

  That's an excellent/wonderful choice.

  No problem.

  Sure.

  Coming right up.

  You got it!

— *Note* —

 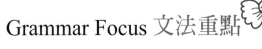 
1. We stop to serve breakfast at 7 in the morning.
2. We stop serving breakfast at 7 in the morning.

上述兩個句子，稍不留神很可能會造成認知上的混淆：

「我們早上七點開始供應早餐。」
「我們早上七點停止供應早餐。」

類似的動詞用法還有：

3. Remember to change the menu when you leave.
4. I remember changing the menu when I left.

「記得在離開時更換菜單。」
「我記得在離開時更換了菜單。」

5. I forgot to turn off the light when I left the restaurant.
6. I forgot turning off the light when I left the restaurant.

「我在離開餐廳時忘了關燈。」
「我忘了在離開餐廳時已關了燈。」

上述三個動詞，在其後加動名詞或加不定詞會造成意義上很大的差距。
所以在使用時一定要留意。

Drills & Exercises

—— 練習 ——

Problem Solving:

1. You want to arrange a business breakfast for yourself and representatives of another company. Call the restaurant to reserve a table for the number of people and time you want. Ask what they have on their breakfast menu.

2. Ask someone about their favorite breakfast dishes. Find dishes on the menu that are similar or have some of the same ingredients. Write descriptions of your favorite dishes.

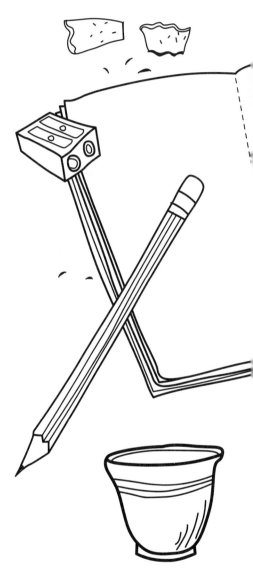

Sample breakfast menu:

Breakfast Buffet $ 13.99

- Farm Fresh Eggs & Omelettes Made To Order
- Savory Breakfast Meats
- Breakfast Potatoes
- Fresh Pastries
- Bagels
- Fresh Made Pancake
- Assorted Cold Cereals
- Fresh Fruit
- Yogurt Bar

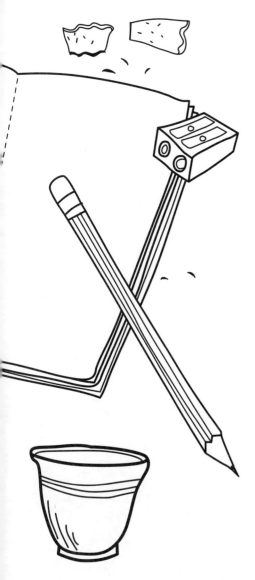

- Coffee, Tea, Orange Juice, Milk, Smoothies, & Juice

Continental Buffet: $ 9.50

Fresh pastries, bagels, assorted cold cereals, fresh fruit, yogurt bar and choice of coffee, tea, milk, juice or Pepsi products

Amazing Omelettes:

(Served with hash brown and you choice of buttermilk pancake or wheat toast. Substitute fresh fruit in place of toast $2.)

Ham & Cheese Omelette $ 9

Hormel Cure ham and melted cheddar cheese

Garden Fresh Omelette $ 9

Fresh mushrooms, tomatoes, onions, green peppers, spinach and cheddar cheese

Denver Omelette $ 10

Onions, green peppers, diced ham and cheddar cheese

Asparagus & Bacon Omelette $ 9

Fresh asparagus, smoked bacon, tomato and feta cheese

說到早餐，蛋類食品應該是每個人最先想到的食材：

- 炒蛋（scrambled eggs）：將兩個或兩個以上的蛋（歐美人士對所使用的蛋的數量是一點也不吝嗇）輕輕打散（lightly beaten），加上牛奶或水，炒時不斷攪拌（stir）。若喜歡鬆一點的蛋可強調 "soft and fluffy"（鬆散）；若希望硬一點就說 "well done"（老一點）。
- 煎蛋／荷包蛋（fried eggs）：用牛油、食用油或乳瑪琳／人造奶油（margarine）煎整個蛋。煎蛋時因火候的不同又可分成；

  over hard/over-hard：兩面煎，蛋黃（yolk）要煎老些硬些。

  over medium：兩面煎，蛋黃變稠但仍會流動。

  over easy /sunny side down：兩面煎，蛋黃要嫩且會流動。在不同地區會用不同的說法："dippy eggs," "dip eggs," "treasure eggs."

  sunny side up：太陽蛋；通常只煎一面，蛋黃呈液體狀；有時會在煎的那一面上澆（baste）油脂以免焦了。有時也被稱為 "eggs up."

  fried：兩面煎，在煎時把蛋黃打散並讓它變硬。通常用在煎蛋三明治上。
- 煮蛋（boiled egg）：將連殼的蛋放入沸騰的水中；若要全熟（hard-boiled eggs）時，將蛋白和蛋黃煮到全熟，通常要 15 分鐘左右；若喜歡半生不熟的（soft-boiled eggs），則要 3-10 分鐘不等。煮全熟的蛋比半熟的蛋要容易多了！
- 水煮荷包（poached eggs）：將蛋殼拿掉後，用水煮蛋同樣的方式和時間要求，但是用熱水而非滾水中所煮出來的蛋。
- 蛋捲（omelet）：用煎鍋將打好的蛋用牛油或食用油去煎。因中間通常有不同的餡（fillings），所以要將蛋對摺起來；有時，也會在蛋捲的表面上用些不同的裝飾（topping）。有人說成功的蛋捲是用全熟的炒蛋所包起來的半熟炒蛋！
- 班乃迪克蛋（Eggs Benedict）：用兩個切半的英式鬆餅（English muffins）上放置水煮荷包蛋和煙燻豬肉（back bacon/Canadian bacon）並淋上荷蘭醬（hollandaise sauce 用蛋黃奶油和檸檬汁所調製而成微酸的醬料）。

誰說吃蛋容易呢？

Note

Unit
6

Snails? I'll pass. (Appetizers) Food orders
點餐（前菜）

Appetizers (開胃菜, 小菜) are finger food usually served prior to (在…之前) a meal, or in between mealtimes, and are also called hors d'oeuvres, antipasti, or starters, and may range from the very simple to the very complex, depending on the occasion (場合) and the time devoted to making them. They are typically savory (鹹的; 美味的) instead of sweet and served in portions small enough for people to consume in one or two bites (口). Appetizers are a common accompaniment (附加物) to aperitifs (飯前酒), cocktails (雞尾酒) served prior to a meal. At dinners, banquets (宴會) and the like (類似的事物), appetizers may be served before a meal. This is especially common at weddings, when it takes time for the wedding party and the guests to get to a reception (酒會, 茶會) after marriage has taken place; guests and family members can nibble on (輕咬, 啃) them while waiting for the main courses (主菜). Appetizers may also be served at long parties that occur after a regular meal time; a mid-afternoon party where there is no intent to (無意) serve dinner or an evening party that occurs after dinner so that guests can have the opportunity to snack (吃點心). They're an especially good idea when guests are consuming alcohol, since they help to cut down (減少) on alcohol absorption (吸收). Additionally, many restaurants feature a range of appetizers that are ordered just prior to a meal as a first course.

Eating small portions of food dates back (回溯) centuries and was practiced (實行) by many early civilizations. The tapas of Spain were introduced by King Alfonso the 10th, who suffered from a stomach ailment (胃痛) that necessitated (使…成必須) eating small portions. The term *hors d'oeuvre* is French for "outside the works" and originally referred to buildings outside a main structure (建築物); it is now a common culinary phrase (烹飪用語) for small food served outside the main meal. How extensive appetizers selections are depends on the setting (背景). If they are meant to stimulate (刺激) the appetite before a main meal, they are typically light and limited. Conversely (相反地), appetizers served at cocktail parties are more bountiful (豐富) and heavier (油膩) as they replace a meal such as lunch and decelerate (減低) the effects of alcohol. Appetizers can be as simple as chips (洋芋片) and dip (沾醬) or bowls of roasted nuts (堅果) or extravagant (奢華的) concoctions (混合) of meat, seafood and exotic (異國情調的) cheeses, fruits and vegetables. Mixing hot and cold hors d'oeuvres is common as is offering low calories selections alongside more indulgent (放縱的) ones. Buffets are good ways to present appetizers as people can serve themselves and socialize (社交) while making selections. More formal setting have a waiting (服務) staff offering hors d'oeuvres to guests on platters (大盤子) or at serving stations (工作站). Since people are generally mobile (活動的) while consuming appetizers,

keep the selections simple to eat with fingers and avoid sauces and gravies (醬汁) that create spills (溢濺) and drips (流落).

Appetizers come in many types:

Canapés (開胃小菜): They are usually small pieces of toast, bread or crackers topped with a savory combination of food.

Vegetable Appetizers (混合蔬菜): Vegetables are used as a base for other foods; they are either thickly sliced to form a base, or stuffed with fillings (填料).

Hot Appetizers (熱開胃菜): Hot appetizers are items, such as mini quiches, bruschetta and puffed pastry envelopes, stuffed with savory fillings.

Dips and Spreads (醬汁塗料開胃菜): They are paired with a variety of raw vegetables, bread pieces, crackers or corn chips. The vegetables or other foods are usually dunked into the dip and then eaten. You can also spread the dip into small pieces of bread or crackers.

Fish and Meat Appetizers (肉類開胃菜): Chickens wings, asparagus wrapped in bacon, warm sausage slices, small crabs or slices of smoked salmon, they tend to be filling (飽實的), so serve them in fairly small quantities.

Glossary: Words you can use 詞彙

———○———

amuse-bouche	法式開胃小點；取悅嘴巴的開胃小菜
antipasto (sing.)/antipasti (pl.)	義大利開胃涼菜
appetite	胃口
appetizer	開胃菜
aperitif/digestif	飯前 / 後酒
asparagus	蘆筍

B

banquet	宴會
baked barbequed pork cake	叉燒酥
BBQ pork rice roll	叉燒腸粉
bite (n.)	一口的分量
bountiful	豐富的充足的
bruschetta	普切塔（在烤過且抹了橄欖油的麵包上加料）
Buffalo chicken wings	水牛城辣雞翅

C

call for	需要（飲料）
champagne	香檳
canapés	法式小點
calories	卡洛里，熱量

chip	洋芋片，（英）炸馬鈴薯條
carrot and celery sticks	紅蘿蔔和芹菜條
cheese/chocolate fondue	起司／巧克力小火鍋
chicken tenders	雞柳條
chicken nuggets	雞塊
cocktail	雞尾酒
consume	消耗，吃光喝完
combo	混合，綜合
crab cake	蟹肉餅
crackers	薄餅乾
cut down	減少

D

delicious	美味的
delicacy	佳餚
Dim Sum	粵式點心
Di Jon mustard	歐式芥末醬
dip	沾醬
drip	滴下來

E

egg roll	春捲（也有人說 spring roll）
escargot	烤田螺
extravagant	奢侈的，豪華的

exotic	異國情調的，外來的

F

filled	填塞
fillings	填塞料
finger food	可用手取食小份量的食品
fried calamari	炸魷魚（花枝或墨魚 squid/cuttle-fish）
fried mozzarella sticks	炸起司條

G

gravy	肉汁，滷
guacamole	酪梨醬
give something a try	姑且一試

H

hors d'oeuvre	開胃小菜，冷盤
horseradish	辣根

K

ketchup	番茄醬

M

mozzarella sticks	起司條
mustard	芥茉醬

N

nacho	墨西哥脆餅
nibble	一點一點地咬或吃

O

olives	橄欖
oysters Rockefeller	生蠔

P

pastry envelope	如韭菜盒子形狀般的糕點
pate	法式雞肝；肉醬
pizza bites	小披薩
platter	大淺盤
portion	份量
promote	升遷
potato skins	烤馬鈴薯皮
pot stickers	鍋貼
prior to	在…之前
puffed	蓬鬆的

Q

quiche	加餡的乳蛋餅；鹹派

R

raw	生的
roasted nuts	香烤堅果

S

salsa	莎莎醬；任何醬料
sauce	以番茄和辣椒做成的基醬
serving station	工作區；提供餐飲的地點
set one heart/mind on	下定決心
Shao Mai (open-face steamed dumplings)	燒賣
shrimp cocktail	番茄調味醬沾蝦
sommelier	酒侍
smoked salmon	煙燻鮭魚
soft shell crab	炸軟殼蝦
spill	灑出來
spoil	糟蹋，損壞
spread	鋪抹的塗料
steamed BBO pork bun	叉燒包
stuffed mushroom	鑲蘑菇
sufficient	足夠

T

tapas	西班牙小菜
taro cake	芋頭糕
tempt	引誘，打動
That's the thought!	本意（如此）
tortilla roll-ups	薄玉米捲餅
Turnip Radish Cake	蘿蔔糕

W

wedding party/reception	婚禮

What to Say 情境對話

———○———

Situational Dialogue 1

🔅 6-1

S (Sommelier): Good evening. It's nice to see you again.

C (Customer): Thank you. It's good to be back again.

S Would you care for an aperitif before your meal?

C Yes, I think we would. As matter of fact, today we have something to celebrate. I've just been promoted to Regional Sales Manager.

S That's wonderful! Congratulations, sir!

C I think that calls for something special. What would you recommend?

S How about some champagne? And I would also recommend an amuse-bouche of crackers, cheese, pate, and olives.

C Excellent! I think that's just what we are going to order.

S Very good, sir. Some champagne and amuse-bouche for both of you.

Situational Dialogue 2

🔅 6-2

W (Waiter): How are you this evening? Care for some appetizers for starters?

C (Customer): That sounds like a good idea. I think we'll start with an order of fried calamari and a shrimp cocktail.

W I'm sorry, but we are out of the shrimp cocktail at the moment. Would you like to have something else instead?

C Is that so? I kind of had my heart set on the shrimp cocktail. What would you

recommend?

W The oysters Rockefeller would be a good bet; they're fresh and delicious.

C Are they raw or cooked?

W They are raw and served with cocktail sauce, which is a combination of ketchup, horseradish, and Dijon mustard.

C All right. I'll give it a try.

W How about some aperitifs?

C I think we'll pass. Appetizers will be sufficient.

Situational Dialogue 3 6-3

C Excuse me. What's in the combo platter?

W (Waitress): Our appetizer combo platter has potato skins, hot and spicy Buffalo wings, fried mozzarella sticks, and carrot and celery sticks.

C That sounds very bountiful; I sure hope that won't spoil my appetite!

W Well, our servings are rather big; perhaps you can share the appetizers between you two?

C That's the thought. OK, we'll have one of your house appetizer combo platters. Also, how about some of your house white wine to wash it down?

W You want your wine by the bottle or by the glass?

C How about two house whites by the glass?

W One combo platter and two house whites coming right up.

Situational Dialogue 4

 6-4

W (Waitress): Can I tempt your gents (gentlemen) with some of our appetizers?

C I thought we were going to have Dim Sum for dinner tonight.

W We offer a wide variety of Cantonese dishes for you to choose from, and, naturally, you can either have Dim Sum as the main course or a starter.

C Is that a fact? Let's see what's on the menu. What the difference between a BBQ bun and a BBQ cake?

W The BBQ bun is steamed and the BBQ cake is baked. They are both very tasty.

C Then, we'll have one of each. We also would like to have an order of turnip cake and pot stickers.

W Well, if I may, I think that might be too much. I mean, you don't to want to ruin your appetite.

C I think you're right. Cancel the pot stickers so we can some room left in our stomachs for other delicacies.

How to Say It 句型介紹

———○———

Followings are some useful expressions you can use when ordering appetizers:

- 推薦

  Our ___ (chocolate/cheese fondue, ...) is out of this world!

  Our chef highly recommends ___ (tarot cake, ...).

  The Gourmet Reviews (老饕評論) ranked our ____ (pot stickers, ...)as one of the top 3 in town.

  If you have a sweet tooth, you'll love our ___ (甜的開胃小點).

- 作法

  The ___ (nachos, ...) come with salsa and a guacamole dip.

  The ___ (stuffed mushroom, ...) is stuffed with ___ (pork, beef, ...)

  The ___ (fries, ...) is topped with ___ (melt cheese, ...).

- 提醒是否點太多

  Our serving is rather big; maybe you would like to reconsider your orders?

  The portion is gigantic in our restaurant; are you sure you want to order that many?

  I am sure you won't want to miss our other specialties because you have one appetizer too many.

- 飯前酒

  Would you care for some ___ (vermouth 苦艾酒 , champagne 香檳 , fino 最高品質的雪莉酒 , amontillado 一般雪莉酒) for your aperitif?

  How about something to go with your appetizers?

Grammar Focus 文法重點

———— o ————

兩個或兩個以上的主詞用 or, either...or..., neither...not..., mot only...but (also)... 連接時，動詞須與最靠近的主詞一致：

▶ Either Jack or I am going to apply for the opening in the restaurant.
  Jack 或我裡面有一個人會去申請餐館的工作。

▶ Not only the owner but also his staff are all friendly.
  不僅老闆，連他的員工都十分友善。

▶ Is the waitress or the waiter to be blamed?
  是女侍者還是男侍者該被責備？

▶ Not you but I am to be blamed.
  不是你是我該受責備。

兩個主詞由 as well as, not less than, together with, along with, but, except, like 等連接時，動詞要和第一個主詞一致：

▶ The chef as well as his helpers is told to wash their hands before start working.
  廚師和幫手們都被告知在開始工作前要洗手。

▶ Mary no less than Jack is a food server.
  瑪莉和傑克一樣是好侍者。

▶ The safe together with the money in it was stolen from the restaurant last night.
  餐廳的保險箱和裡面的錢昨晚一起被偷了。

▶ The waiters and waitresses like their captain are dressed in white uniform.
  男侍者女侍者和他們的領班都穿著白制服。

—— 練習 ——

Work with a partner and turn turns being a server and a customer to practice the following scenario. Make sure that both of you use vocabulary you learned in this unit.

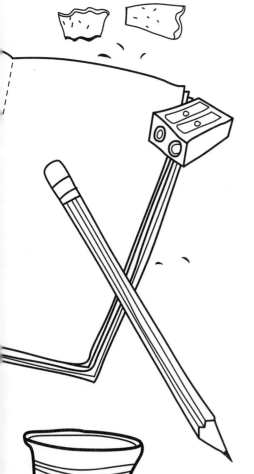

- A server welcomes a guest and asks if he/she would like to order an appetizer. Make suggestions to encourage customer to order.

- The customer should use the provided menu as a reference and ask questions about the appetizers. The customer is not to choose what the server recommends first.

Some words and expressions to help you:

crispy, juicy, fresh, tasty, quite, fairly, out of this world

- Is/Are... good?

- How does ... taste like?

- What is ...?

- Do you recommend ...?

Suggested menu for appetizers:

Shrimp Cocktail   **market price**

Stuffed Mushrooms   **$ 2.25 per person**

Stuffed with cheese and Spanish

Add crab for $0.50 per person

Chicken Kebob   **$ 2.95 per person**

Grilled chicken, onions, peppers

and mushrooms

Fried Wings   **$ 2.75 per person**

Chicken wings and drums

Honey Brown BBQ Wings   **$ 2.85 per person**

Chicken wings and drums smothered in

our honey BBQ sauce and grilled to perfection

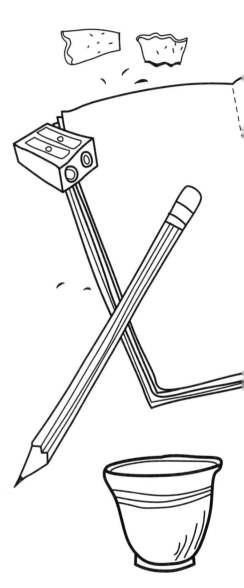

西荣的午晚餐大多由下列幾個部分組成：

- 麵包類：bun, roll
- 開胃品前菜：一般有甜（sweet）但多數爲鹹（savory），有熱食（hot appetizers）也有冷食（cold appetizers），有生的（raw）也有熟的（cooked）
- 湯類：有濃湯（bisque/pottage/thick soup）和清湯（consommé/clear soup/clear borsch）
- 沙拉：一般可分爲水果沙拉（fruit salad）、蔬菜素沙拉（vegetable salad）和葷沙拉（meat salad）。常見的如：Mixed Salad（什錦沙拉）。Chef Salad（主廚沙拉），Seafood salad（海鮮沙拉）等。
- 主菜（entrée/main course）：也有人稱主盤，多以海鮮和禽畜肉爲主要食材，用炸烤烘煮蒸和燒等方式製作而成。
- 奶酪 / 起司和甜點：主菜用完後即上甜點（dessert），但有些餐廳會問清楚是否要在餐後上奶酪或起司；若要，先上奶酪後上甜點。吃起司或奶酪通常會配上麵包或薄脆餅乾（crackers）芹菜條（celery sticks）。甜點則又有冷熱之分如 ice cream, pudding（布丁）、蛋奶素（soufflé）、派（pie）、果凍（jelly）和蛋糕。

在飯前或搭配開胃品的酒類多以雪莉酒（sherry）或苦艾酒（vermouth）爲主；
和魚或家禽搭配的酒習慣上多以白酒（white wine）和玫瑰紅（rose）爲主；
和乳酪起司牛排烤肉和其他肉類的搭配多以紅酒（red wine）爲主；
和甜品搭配的酒則多以香檳（champagne）或甜葡萄酒（sweet wine）爲主，
不過香檳酒通常可以和任何菜搭配。

Unit
7

When the East meets the West I
(Cuisines of the World) 點餐（正餐）

Few cuisines (菜餚,烹飪) are rated (排行) as the best cuisines of the world because they comprise of (構成) numerous exclusive (獨一無二) dishes, mix (混合體) of lovely ingredients (食材) and definite symphonies (和諧) of flavors. Here are some finger-licking (好吃) cuisines that have topped (居首) the list of the world best cuisines.

Undoubtedly, French cuisine tops the list of the world-best cuisines; though it has not achieved the popularity of the Chinese and Italian cuisines, their restaurants are among the finest in the world and they have influenced many cuisines all over the world. In the 21st century, this delectable (甘美的) cookery (烹調術) can be called as "haute cuisine (高級烹飪術)." French epicurean (愛好美食) is incomplete without pastries (糕點), cheese and wine, being perhaps the most famous of all. In Paris alone, there are over 5,000 eating spots to binge (大吃大喝), with menus and prices suiting (適合) everybody.

The Italian cuisine is one of the oldest gourmets (美味佳餚) in the world, and pizzas and pasta (義大利麵食) have contributed to make this one of the world's most popular

cuisines. The Italian platters (盤餐) highlighted (強調) the beautiful savors (風 味) of potatoes, pepper and corn in food. An Italian meal is broken down into several sections: antipasto (the appetizer (前菜)), primo, (pasta or rice dish), secondo (meat course), dolce (dessert). Italy is also renowned for making over 400 kinds of cheese, including the famous Parmigianino Reggiano, and 300 types of delicious sausages (臘腸 , 香腸).

There is probably a Chinese restaurant in every part of the world, and every country has adapted this cuisine to suit their particular taste buds. Chinese noodles and fried rice have become a part of the weekly menus in many homes. Originated in various parts of China and now spread throughout the world, the Chinese cuisine is now eaten by a third of the world's population every day. What makes this cuisine so special and well-known? Its recipes are easy, instant, economical and tasty. The true Chinese food fans have even learned how to eat with chopsticks to get the true Chinese experience. However, some dishes are cooked from endangered species, such as facai moss (髮菜) while others from meat that you would want to avoid such as dog.

One of the world's most sophisticated (複雜) and diverse (多樣的) cuisine, the Indian cuisine is quite popular for its seasoning (調味料) and amazing flavors (風味, 味道). The ever popular chicken curry and chicken tikka masala (串烤咖哩雞) are among the world's most popular dishes. Only a part of the Indian cuisine is known to the world, and most people in the world associated it with just curry and biryani (香料飯) and naan (烤餅), which are basically recipes from the northern region of India. The mouth-watering (垂涎的, 好吃的) Indian cuisine is divided into four categories: North, South, East and West. With the growing number of Indian restaurants everywhere, people are becoming to sample food such as dosas (扁豆薄餅) from the south, pohe (糙米, 薏仁) from the west and maach (魚類料理) from the east. Most of the dishes are vegetarian, but many include lamb, goat, chicken, meat and even fish. Indian cuisine is usually very spicy; so in order to enjoy the food, start slowly and in a few weeks you will get accustomed to Indian Palates (味覺).

Glossary: Words you can use 詞彙

———— ○ ————

Below is a list of dishes commonly found in Japanese cuisine:

- Rice dishes:
  rice porridge (粥)
  rice bowl (蓋飯)
  sushi (壽司)

- **men-rui** (noddles 麵)

- **agemono** (deep-fried dishes 炸物)
  yakimono (grilled and pan-fried dishes 燒物)
  nebemono (one pot cooking 鍋物)
  nimono (stewed dishes 煮物)
  itamemono (stir-fried dishes 炒物)
  sashimi (raw fish 生魚片)
  suimono/shirumono (soups 湯 / 汁物)
  tsukemono (pickled or salted foods 漬物)

- **pan** (bread 麵包)
  wagashi (Japanese-style sweets 和菓子)
  dagashi (old fashioned Japanese-style sweets 御菓子)
  yogashi (Western-style sweets 洋菓子)

A

allergic to	對…過敏
alternative	另個選擇
arcade	長廊商場
assorted	綜合的
as well	也…

B

batter	麵糊
be in for a treat	會喜歡的
be keen on	渴望
be longing for	想…

C

ceramic shop	陶器店
china	瓷器
commonly	普遍地
crispy	酥脆的
custard	蛋奶凍，(烤牛奶雞蛋) 布丁，加雞蛋、牛奶焙烤、蒸煮，成凍型的食品

D

definite	一定的，明確的
Do in Rome as Romans do	入境隨俗
dressing	沙拉醬，調料

E

economical	便宜的
endangered spices	瀕臨絕跡邊緣的品種
ever popular	愈來愈受歡迎的

F

flavor	味道，風味

G

gingko nuts	銀杏
glassware	玻璃器皿
go well with...	和⋯很搭配
grated	磨碎的
grilled	烤的，炙的
be leaning toward	傾向

I

be into + something	喜歡⋯

L

lime	萊姆
lobster	龍蝦

N

numerous	極多的

P

palate	上顎； 味覺 (也有人會用 taste bud 味蕾來形容)

| prawn | (英)蝦；(美)shrimp 有人會依大 (prawn) 小 (shrimp) 來區分 |
| prefer A to B | 喜歡 A 勝過 B |

R

radish	小紅蘿蔔 (horseradish: 辣根)
region	地區
refreshing	清涼的，提神的
rest	座，臺，架
Japanese sake	日本清酒

S

salmon	鮭魚
sample	品嘗
soy sauce/soybean sauce	醬油
subtle	微妙的，深奧的

T

| tempting | 誘人 |
| testbud | 味蕾 |

U

| unusual | 非比尋常的 |

What to Say 情境對話

─────○─────

Situational Dialogue 1   7-1

W (Waiter): Good evening. Are you ready to order, sir?

G (Guest): Yes. What kind of food is the tempura (天婦羅)?

W It is fish, prawns and assorted vegetables dipped in batter and then deep fried until crispy. It's very popular with both Japanese and foreign customers.

G Um. It sure sounds delicious and tempting. We'll have the tempura dinner for two, if you please.

W Very good, sir. The dinner comes with raw fish. Will that be OK?

G We are really not that into raw fish. Can we have something else instead?

W In that case, I would recommend the Chawanmushi (茶碗蒸蛋). It's an egg custard with chicken, shrimp and gingko nuts.

G OK, we will try that.

Situational Dialogue 2   7-2

W This is the sauce for the tempura. Please mix the grated radish with the soy sauce and then dip it in before eating.

G Thanks very much. By the way, what is this thing under the chopsticks?

W It's a chopstick rest. We use it so that the tips of the chopsticks do not touch the table.

G I see. Where can I get these?

W There is a ceramics shop in the Arcade, They can also be purchased at any glassware or china shop.

G They will definitely make good presents back home.

Situational Dialogue 3   7-3

W Good evening. A table for two?

G Yes, please.

W Would you prefer to sit at a table or at the counter?

G The counter will be fine. We'd like to watch how the food's being prepared. After all, we are in a teppanyaki restaurant.

W Yes, sir. You are in for a treat of grilled meat, prawns and vegetables dishes which are prepared in front of the guest. What would you like to drink?

G What kind of cocktails do you have?

W I'm afraid we don't serve cocktails here. We have beer, wine, or Japanese sake.

G "When in Rome do as the Romans do." We'll have the sake.

Situational Dialogue 4

C (Chef): Good evening, ma'am. Your lobster and King Salmon.

G That looks good.

C Would you prefer mixed sauce or Japanese dressing?

G What's in the Japanese dressing?

C It's made of lime juice, vinegar and soy sauce. It has a very subtle and refreshing flavor and taste as well.

G We will try it then.

C It goes very well with seafood or fish. How is it?

G Excellent. A very unusual taste.

C Thank you, ma'am.

How to Say It 句型介紹

——— ○ ———

Followings are some useful expressions you can use when ordering main course:

- 詢問

    How does ... taste like?

    What does ... look like?

    How is ... made of?

    What is/are the ingredient (s)?

    I am allergic to ... Is there any ... in it?

- 徵求意見

    What will your recommend?

    What will you choose if you were I?

    What's your favorite?

    Will you take/order... instead of...?

    What's the/my alternative?

- 表示決定

    I'm leaning toward choosing...

    I'm keen on having...

    I have longing for... for a long time.

    I'll pass. (放棄)

    I'll skip it this time. (下次再選)

    I'll take your word for it. (你說了算數)

Grammar Focus 文法重點

———○———

片語在英文中一直有它不可忽視的份量；在本單元情境對話中 "You are in for a treat of..." 就是一個最好的例子。實際上，越是簡單的片語，越有意想不到的效果。試以介系詞 in, on 及 at 為例，就能找到相當生動有趣的片語使用：

In:

in the ball park: 在預算範圍內

A proposal in the ball park of $50,000 is manageable. (在五萬塊錢預算內的可接受。)

be in for: 一定會⋯

He behaved badly and is in for a beating. (他行為惡劣一定會被處罰。)

We are in for a long rainy season. (我們一定會有個長雨季。)

the ins and outs: 詳情

There will definitely be an uproar (騷動) once the ins and outs of the kidnapping (綁架) come out (真相大白).

On:

on and on: 繼續的

He repeated the same story on and on without even a pause (暫停).

on to...: 精通；知曉

He was really on to something when writing that report. (他在寫報導時還真得知道些內幕。)

on loan to: 借調

Some government officials are on loan from schools. (一些政府官員是由學校借調過來的。)

At:

at the first sight: 第一眼

It's love at the first sight for the newly wed when they first met. (新婚夫婦第一次見面就一見
鍾情。)

be at: 意欲

What are you at? (你想要做什麼 ?)

— *Note* —

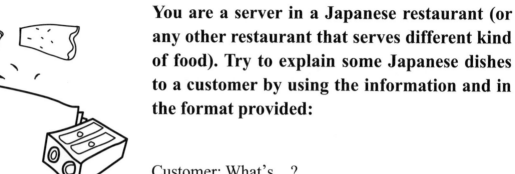

Drills & Exercises

——練習——

You are a server in a Japanese restaurant (or any other restaurant that serves different kind of food). Try to explain some Japanese dishes to a customer by using the information and in the format provided:

Customer: What's ...?
Server: ... is ...

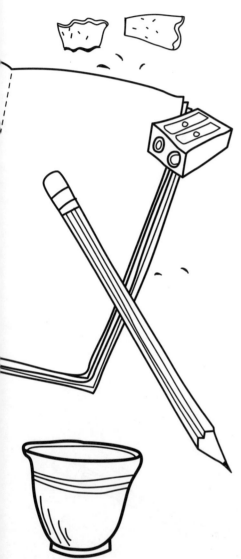

- Curry rice (咖哩飯): Introduced from the UK in the late 19th century and is now one of the most popular dishes Japan. It's much milder (溫和) than its Indian counterpart (咖哩；相對應的人事物).

- Kamameshi (釜飯): Rice topped with (覆蓋) vegetagbles and chicken or seafood, then baked (烘烤) in an individual-sized (個人份) pot (鍋).

- Zosui/Ojiya (雜炊): It is a soup containing rice stewed (煮燉) in stock (原汁，湯汁), often with egg, meat, seafood, vegetables or mushroom, and flavored with (調味) with miso or soy.

- Sushi: It is a vinegared rice (醋飯) or mixed with various fresh ingredients (生食材), usually seafood or vegetables.

- Ramen: It is the thin light yellow noodles served in hot chicken or pork broth (高湯) with various toppings（澆料）. It's of Chinese origin and a popular item in Japan.

- Karrage（唐揚，炸物）: Bite-size（一口咬）pieces of chicken, fish, octopus（章魚）or other meat. Floured（沾麵粉）and deep fried.

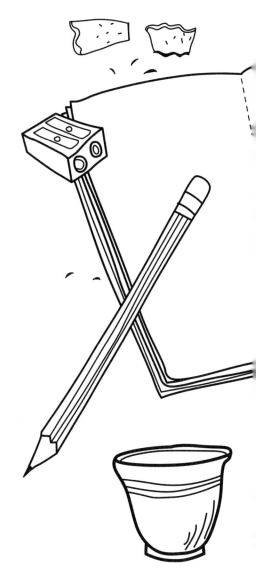

　　放眼台灣，各式各樣日本拉麵店林林總總；有強調湯頭、麵和叉燒的一風堂拉麵；有強調隱私，自己在自己封閉位置上進食的一蘭拉麵；有堅持完美湯頭否則今天不營業的赤鬼／幌屯拉麵，有以日本電視拉麵冠軍達人為活廣告的赤坂拉麵；有強調台灣風味的味千拉麵，更有以大骨熬湯為訴求的博多拉麵！若以口味來區分，有胡麻味噌、有豚骨、有醬油還有地獄拉麵。有人為了要一快朵頤，情願排隊（to stay in line）也不放棄。就好像很多人，不管身分不論場合，只要是流行就一定要具有的名牌（brand-name）皮包，或是不管胖瘦不分年齡大家都要穿的（one size fits all）的服飾；究竟飲食男女（the ordinary people）所在意的是需求還是把物質產品當作身分地位象徵（symbol of status）？

　　社會學者馬斯洛（A. Maslow）所提出的人類五大需求（生理、安全、歸屬、尊重和自我實現）詳實地描述了人性；吃日式拉麵是為了填飽肚子，還是要能讓自己身體健康有保障？是要將自己歸屬在哈日一族，還是覺得只有如此才能得到他人尊重？當然，吃拉麵和自我實現這個需求的最高境界實在很難扯上關係；我對自己的期許要靠吃拉麵來證實和實現嗎？

　　吃在英文可說成 eat，如同在 eat one's humble pie（忍氣吞聲，認錯），也可說成 devour 如同在 to devour one's food（狼吞虎嚥），當然也能說成 savor（品味）如同在 to savor flavors in life（品嘗人生百味）。同樣是吃但效果期許不同；看來吃還真是一門大學問呢！

Unit
8

When the East meets the West II
(Cuisines of the World) 點餐（正餐）

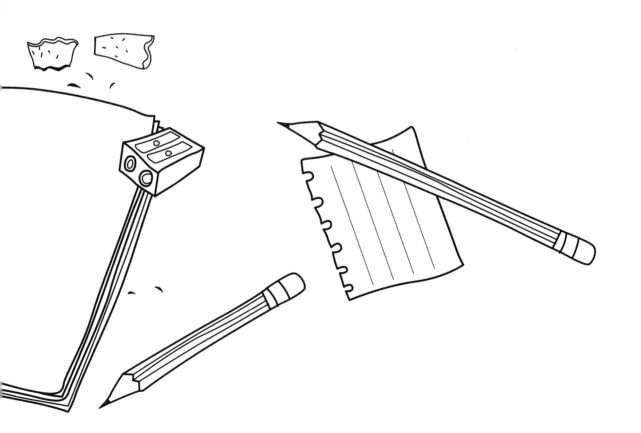

Read 閱讀

Many people tend to equate Thai food with Chinese food, but there is a world of difference between the two. The Thai green and red curries are very popular and their balanced (均衡) fusion (融合) of hot, sour and sweet ingredients makes for great combinations. True Thai food is made with fresh herbs (芳草藥草) and rice is one of their main staples (主食).

A sangria (汽酒名稱) accompanying (伴隨) the delicious variety of Spanish food is one of the joys of this world. Spanish cooking is mainly done with olive oil (橄欖油), and the diverse (多元, 多樣) assortment (綜合) of seafood available, and the range of Tapas (餐前小菜) offered as an appetizers have all contributed towards the popularity of this cuisine.

Lightly cooked with a minimal number of spices and ingredients, Japanese cooking is rapidly becoming all the rage (風行一時). Judging from its popularity their signature (代表性的) dish seems to be sushi, but there are many other dishes which have become part of folklore (傳奇傳說).

There is really no benchmark (基準) for American cuisine, but with the popularity of burgers and fried chicken and apple pies, American cuisine has also become very popular over the world. Most of these have achieved their fame (名聲) due to the advent of (到來) fast food chains which have traversed across (穿越, 橫過) the nations. You may not feel it is the world's best food, but it certainly is among the most sought after (找尋).

Glossary: Words you can use 詞彙

———○———

Below is a list of everyday names of Dim Sum:

- Steamed bun

  Steamed egg custard bun（奶皇包）

  Steamed lotus seed paste and egg yolk bun（蛋黃蓮蓉包）

  Steamed barbecued pork bun（叉燒包）

  Steamed vegetable and meat bun（菜肉包）

- Steamed salty dim sum

  Steamed chicken feet/pork ribs with black bean sauce（鼓汁蒸鳳爪／排骨）

  Steamed fresh shrimp dumpling（蝦餃）

  Steamed stuffed dumplings with shrimp/Siu mai（燒賣）

  Turnip cake (steamed/pan-fried)（蒸／煎蘿蔔糕）

- Steamed rice-roll

  Steamed rice-roll with beef（牛肉腸粉）

  Steamed rice-roll with vegetarian stuffing（蒸羅漢齋腸粉）

- Pan-fried and deep-fried（煎／炸）dim sum

  Spring roll（春捲）

  Deep fried wonton（炸餛飩）

  Pan-fried/seared beancurd sheet roll（煎豆腐捲）

  Pan-fried sweetness water chestnut cake（煎馬蹄條）

- Dessert

  Red/Mung bean sweet soup（紅／綠豆湯）

  Egg tart（蛋撻）

The followings are some everyday Chinese dishes:

- Chow mein (炒麵)

- Fried rice (炒飯)

- Noodle soup (湯麵)

- Mapo tofu (麻婆豆腐)

- Sweet and sour pork (咕咾肉，糖醋肉)

- Twice cooked pork (回鍋肉)

- Century egg (皮蛋)

- Soy/Tea egg (滷 / 茶葉蛋)

- Buddha's delight (羅漢齋)

- Pickled vegetables (醬菜)

- Fried/Steamed/Boiled dumplings (鍋貼 / 蒸餃 / 水餃)

- Steamed bun with fillings (包子)

- Steamed bun (饅頭)

- Zongzi (glutinous rice (糯米) wrapped in bamboo leaves with a savory or sweet filling) (粽子)

- Scallion pancakes (蔥油餅)

- Shaobing (a flaky (扁平) baked or pan-seared (烙燒) dough (麵糰) pastry (燒餅)

- Youtiao/Crullers (long strips of deep fried dough) (油條)

- Congee (Chinese rice porridge) (稀飯)

A

A "must"	一定要⋯的

C

Chinese cabbage	大白菜
chili pepper	辣椒

E

equate	等於

G

gourmet	美食家，老饕
grease	油脂

K

kid	開玩笑

P

portion	（一）份
precise	正是；精準；嚴格
pushcart	推車

S

sauté	炒，煸
serving	(一份)食物或飲料
signature	招牌，代表
specialty	專長，名產，特製品
successively	連續地，依次地

T

to take word right out of one's mouth	正是吾意！

W

wash down	吃下，沖下
wholeheartedly	全心全力的；= heartedly: 由衷的
a world of difference	大不相同

Y

You almost got me there!	差點唬住我了
You can say that again!	說得好！

What to Say 情境對話

---○---

Situational Dialogue 1

 8-1

[S] (Server): Are you folks ready to order?

[G] (Guest): I'm not sure what to order. What is the specialty of this restaurant?

[S] The Kung Bao Chicken is very popular here. I recommend it wholeheartedly.

[G] Kung Bao Chicken? What is it like?

[S] It's a very spicy dish with chicken, peanuts and chili peppers.

[G] That sounds delicious. I think I'll order just that. Any other suggestions?

[S] How about a Sauté Cabbage? It's made of sugar, vinegar and cabbage.

[G] Well, are you sure it's not too much for both of us?

[S] We can always make those a serving for one person only.

Situational Dialogue 2

8-2

[G] In that case, how about some soup?

[S] How about something light? A Vegetable and Tofu Soup maybe?

[G] Excellent. We can use it to wash down the grease we might get from the chicken. Just kidding!

[S] You almost got me there! So, a Kung Bao Chicken, a Sautee Cabbage and a Vegetable and Tofu Soup coming right up.

[G] And a couple of beers when you have the chance, make them two Taiwan Beers.

S I'll bring your beers right away. I would imagine you would like to have rice as well?

G Yes, two bowls of rice, please.

Situational Dialogue 3   🔘 8-3

G1 (Guest1): The place is packed! It's not even the weekend.

G2 (Guest2): As they say, "Follow the locals while looking for something to eat." You don't see that many foreigners here, do you?

G1 Looks like we came to right place. I heard that this restaurant has been ranked as a "must" for gourmets three years in a row.

G2 And they specialize in Dim Sum, a Cantonese style snack. I can't wait to find out what they have in store for us.

G1 Let's wave the waiter over and find out.

G2 You took the words right out of my mouth!

Situational Dialogue 4   🔘 8-4

G What's Dim Sum anyway?

S Dim Sum is a traditional Chinese cuisine, Cantonese cuisine to be precise. It's a variety of foods served successively in small portions.

G Is that right? Can you name just a few?

S Well, you have steamed buns, steamed salty dim sum, steamed rice-rolls, pan-fried and deep-fried dim sum, boiled vegetables with sauces and desserts.

G That's a lot to choose from!

S You can say that again! People usually have dim sum for breakfast, lunch and dinner and any time in between.

G Wow! That's something new to us!

S There will be some pushcarts coming your way soon; pick up whatever dishes you want or like. Or, you can order from the menu.

G Thank you very much.

How to Say It 句型介紹

————o————

● 說明

It's ___ (boiled 煮, stewed 燜、燉、煲, stewed in gravy 滷, simmered 燜、燉, braised 紅燒, barbecued/grilled 燒烤, (stir-)fried (翻)炒, baked 烘, broil 高溫烤, smoked 燻, casserole 砂鍋煲, roasted 燒臘, charred 燒焦, quick boiled 汆燙).

It's ___ (sliced 切片, minced 切碎, smashed 搗爛, shredded 切絲, diced 切丁, filleted 切條/柳, stuffed 釀入, boned 去骨, shelled 剝殼, skinned 剝皮, scaled 去鱗, rinsed 涮, dressed 毛去乾淨)

It's ___ (可用前兩項作法名稱) ___ (in tomato 茄汁, in black bean sauce 豆瓣/豆鼓, in rice wine 醋溜, with fish flavor 以燒魚的材料製作出來的醬料, with sweet and sour 糖醋, in hot sauce 乾燒)

———— *Note* ————

Grammar Focus 文法重點

———○———

"Can't help" 和 "can't help but" (不得不) 在用法上有何不同？
其實把它們分類一下就解決：

can't help but + V
= cannot help + Ving
= have no choice/alternative but + to + V

Since there is little food left, I can't help but go outside to get something to eat.
= I can't help going outside to get something to eat since there is little food left.
= I have no choice but to go outside for there is little food left.

在上述例句中，「因為」的英文用了 "since" 和 "for" 兩個字。
實際上，下列的句子都用到「因為」但請注意到每種說法和用字之間的差異：

Because there is little food left, I have no choice but to go out to get something to eat.
= I have no choice but to go out to get something to eat because there is little food left.
= Since there is little food left, I have no choice but to go to get something to eat.
= I have no choice but to go out to get something to eat for there is little food left.
= As there is little food left, I have no choice but to go out to get something to eat.

因為 "for" 是對等連接詞，它只能放在句中；"because" 是從屬連接詞，所以它所引導的子句可以放前也可置後，但子句在前時，需用逗號和主要句子隔開。"Since" 和 "as" 因是副詞，所以所引導的副詞子句多以置於句前為主。

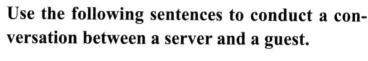

Drills & Exercises

——練習——

Use the following sentences to conduct a conversation between a server and a guest.

Change the roles alternatively.

Guest:

- I am on a diet.

- I had a big ___ (breakfast, lunch) and I need something ___ (light, in small serving)

- I don't know much about ___. What will you recommend?

- What's it like?

- How does it taste?

-

Server:

- Is there anything that you can't or not allowed to eat?

- In that case, how about some ___?

- Actually, we have a wide range of selections you can choose from and you can have the right kind of portion you like.

- Do you like ___ (sweet, salty, spicy, crispy) food?

- Do you like seafood?

- How about___? It's our signature dish.

- It tastes very ___ (tender, strong, aromatic, tasty)

"A man's meat is another's poison," 青菜蘿蔔各有所愛！

　　若說每個人都有愛吃或不愛吃的食物，有喜歡或不喜歡的味道，或可接受或不能接受的飲食習慣實不為過：

- 日本人以清淡、鹹、鮮味為主，不喜歡刺激性強或奇怪的味道。
- 韓國人不喜吃羊肉、香菜以及油膩或味苦的蔬菜；不愛醋、不愛糖更不愛花椒。
- 德國人非常喜歡吃豬肉和各種豬肉製品。喜歡酸白菜和馬鈴薯且每餐飯後必備甜點。
- 英國人用油少、愛清淡，菜量少、質精；不愛過辣或用味精的食物。喝茶一定要加糖和牛奶，一般還得配上茶點或餅乾。
- 法國人愛吃牛、雞、鴨、鵝、蝸牛肉和海鮮，但不吃無鱗魚！口味偏酸甜，講究菜餚的鮮嫩和品質，且葡萄酒是進餐時必備。
- 美國人愛吃甜品和烤炸物。忌食動物內臟也不喜歡帶刺帶骨的食物。不喜歡用毛巾擦手臉！
- 義大利人愛用橄欖油和番茄調味，口味重鹹、鮮、酸辣等重口味的食物和烹調。重原汁原味，不愛動物內臟。

　　你自己知道自己愛或不愛什麼嗎？

Note

Unit

9

Oh, waiter, can I have a refill?
進餐

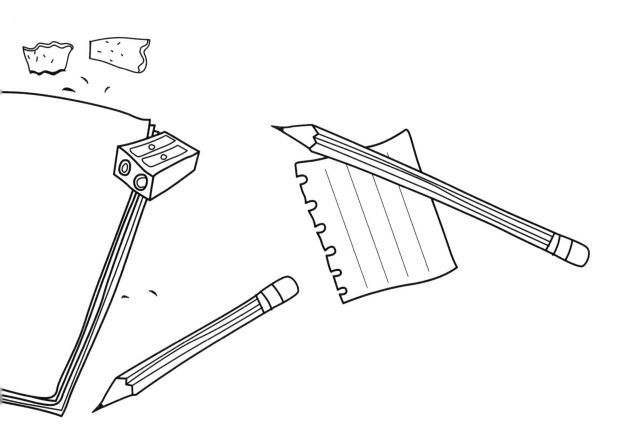

Read 閱讀

———○———

Everybody knows that garlic wards off (避開 , 防止) vampires (吸血鬼) and that spilling (溢出 , 濺出) salt is terrible luck (倒楣 , 厄運). But did you know that you should never cut a banana with a knife? And speaking of knives, did you know that you should never give a knife to a friend? If you're constantly in the kitchen, you should probably consider these superstitions (迷 信) so you don't end up with (以…收場) unmarried, childless, friendless, or worse.

Eggs & Egg Shells

Eggs symbolize (象徵) fertility (生殖力), so farmers would scatter (撒) broken eggs into their fields (田 地) hoping they would bring forth (帶來) an abundant (豐富的 , 大量的) crop (農作物). Also, if you break open an egg and find two yolks (蛋黃), that means someone you know will be getting married or having twins. And when you're cracking (砸開) your egg, make sure to crush (壓 碎) the eggshell (蛋 殼) afterwards; otherwise, legend (傳說) has it, a witch (女巫) will gather up (收集) the pieces, set sail (啓航), and cause terrible storm at sea.

Garlic

Everyone knows that garlic wards off vampires. It can also ward off the curse (詛咒) of the evil eye.

Salt

If you spill salt, you'll get bad luck. To remedy (補救) your misfortune (厄運), throw salt over your left shoulder with your right hand to blind the evil and keep him from taking your soul.

Bread

If you cut open a loaf of bread and see a hole (a.k.a. a large air bubble (空氣 , 氣泡), that means somebody will die soon. The hole in the bread represents a coffin (棺材). You should also cut a cross (十 字 架) into the top of your loaf before baking, otherwise the devil will sit on it and ruin your loaf. Now "hot cross buns" (復活節麵包) makes more sense!

Noodles

In China, long noodles symbolize a long life. So you should never cut your noodles that means you're cutting life short (縮短壽命). Instead you should slurp up (出聲地吸) long noodles up without breaking them.

Tea

Tea, also used in divination (占卜), has lots of superstitions connected to it. For instance, you should never put milk in your tea before the sugar, or you may never get married. Seemingly (表面上) contradictory (矛盾的), undissolved (未溶解 , 未融化的) sugar at the bottom of your cup means someone is in love with you. Spilling your tea means a stranger is about to visit you. And let only one person pour the tea; its' bad luck if the duty is shared.

Coffee

If there are bubbles in your coffee, you should catch them on your spoon and eat them; you'll unexpectedly come into (得到) money.

Oranges

Giving somebody an orange makes them fall in love with you.

Rice

Tossing (丢) rice at a newlywed couple (新婚夫婦) supposedly (據稱) brings the pair good health, wealth, happiness, and prosperity.

Silverware

If you drop a fork, a woman will come to visit. A knife, a man will come to visit. A spoon, a child will come to visit.

Parsley (荷蘭芹，香菜)

Parsley has a surprising number of superstitions around it. Planting (種植) its seeds (種子) will help a woman become pregnant (懷孕), If the plant (植物) thrives (茂盛，繁榮), that means her husband is weak. And whatever you do, don't bring it to a dinner party; giving it as a gift brings bad luck.

Glossary: Words you can use 詞彙

———○———

A	
a.k.a. (= also known an) along with	別名，別稱 和⋯一起

B	
busboy	餐廳雜役

C	
chore come along container consume	瑣事，雜事 進展；一起來 容器 消耗，用光

D	
doggy bag	打包的袋子 (因怕引人側目所以用狗的圖像來轉換注意力)

F	
fish fillet	魚排

G	
go together grilled	相配 烤炙的

L

leftover	吃剩的飯菜

M

melted	融化掉
mess	凌亂
make a mess	弄得一團糟
microwave	微波爐

N

napkin	紙巾

O

on the house	免費
over	烤箱
out-of-this-world	無與倫比的

P

pastries	如水果派等酥皮點心
pitcher	水壺，水罐
pop	(= stick) (快速) 放置

R

refill	續杯
re-heat	重新加熱
round	回合，輪，巡

S

serving spoon	公匙
shaker	鹽 / 胡椒罐
slice (V/N)	片
specifically	特地，明確地
spill	撒出，溢出
sticky	黏
sure thing	沒問題

T

tempt	誘惑
to-go cup	外帶 (紙 / 塑膠) 杯
treat	特別待遇，款待

U

understood	了解 (此處需用過去分詞：「某事讓我知道」)

W

wrap...up	包好

What to Say 情境對話

———○———

Situational Dialogue 1

9-1

S (Server): How is your meal?

G (Guest): Just fine. When you get a chance, can I get another Coke? Refills are on the house, aren't they?

S Yes, sir, they are. Is there anything else?

G How about some more water?

S Sure. I'll bring a pitcher of water along with your refill when I come back.

G Thanks a lot.

S No problem at all.

Situational Dialogue 2

9-2

S Can I clear away these dishes for you, sir?

G That would be nice. Ah, wait! My wife specifically asked me to bring home these leftovers. Can you bring me a doggy bag?

S Certainly, I'd be more than happy to wrap them up for you. Is there anything else you want? How about a dessert? Our chef has prepared some out-of-this world pastries and cakes that will make a perfect ending for your dinner.

G I am sure they are delicious, but no, thanks. Just the check, please.

S Are you sure we can't tempt you with some treats?

G Yes, I'm quite sure. Nice try, though.

Situational Dialogue 3

9-3

G Excuse me. We're going to need another serving spoon here for the soup.

S Right away, ma'am.

G And can I get a glass of apple juice for my daughter? Sorry, that juice needs to be in a to-go cup. Glasses and my five-year old simply do not go together.

S Understood. We usually serve kids' drinks in plastic cups. Anything else?

G Since you asked, how about some extra napkins? With kids, we are sure to spill something.

S Kids will always be kids; don't worry about making a mess. This is a family restaurant, and we have a lot of families here, especially ones with little children.

Situational Dialogue 4

9-4

S How are we doing here? I hope everything is to your satisfaction.

G Everything is great. But is there any chance that you can re-heat my grilled cheese sandwich? You know maybe pop it in the microwave or oven for a couple minutes? I've been busy feeding my kid.

S I'll be happy to do that. We don't use a microwave here, but I'll have the chef put it in the oven for a minute.

G I hope that won't be too much trouble. Can you bake it just long enough so that the cheese melts?

S Sure thing.

How to Say It 句型介紹

———— ○ ————

- 詢問

  How is ___?

  Is ___ the way you wanted it?

  May/Should I ___?

  例：move the plate/shaker... to the side?

  　　cut/slice/serve/mix...for you?

  　　bring more bread sticks/another bread basket/some extra napkins/...for you?

  Will there be anything else?

  So you need anything else?

  How about ___?

  例：another piece of pie for your dessert?

  　　another serving of ...?

- 提醒 / 建議

  The ___ is very ___. Please be careful.

  例：plate/cup/dish...

  　　hot/sticky/full/soft...

  The plate is very hot. Please be careful.

  In my opinion, the ___ simply does not go well with ___.

  The ___ and ___ simply does not match.

  ___ and ___ simply does not go together.

  ___ and ___ will surely go well together.

- 上菜

  Here is your ___. (Please) Enjoy it!

  例：order/steak/fish fillet/salad...

- 提供服務

  I am happy to help.

  I'm at your service.

  There is nothing we can't handle.

  It's no trouble at all.

Grammar Focus 文法重點

———○———

May vs. can

助動詞 can 通常用來表達是否有實際生理能力：

Can you give me a hand?
Can you help me with the luggage?

助動詞 may 則用來徵求許可：

May I come in?
May I try out that pink dress?

實際上，在很多情境中，英文有許多同義字，雖然意思相近，但在使用上還是要謹慎：

He can lift 25 kilos.
He is capable of understanding what the lecture was about.
The young lady is a competent secretary.

第一個例句中，can 用來代表具有的力量；be capable of 則用來表示具理解能力；Competent 則是用來表示具某種專業能力。
就算是反義字，有時他們的意思也不盡然是相反的：

We tried to persuade the boys not to smoke.
We tried to dissuade the boys from smoking.

第一個例句是規勸，第二個例句則是勸阻；若是真的是不規勸，則要養成習慣用 not persuade：

We are not going to persuade the voters to vote for this particular candidate.
也就是說
do/does/did not persuade 不等於 dissuade！

Drills & Exercises

—— 練習 ——

Match the words with their definitions by writing the correct letters into the blanks. The first one is done for you.

___ 1. busboy   ___ 2. doggie bag   ___ 3. pitcher

___ 4. leftovers   ___ 5. refill   ___ 6. napkins

___ 7. to-go cup   ___ 8. shaker

a. something used to put in salt or pepper

b. a cup that is often used when taken out of a restaurant

c. a person who does the chores and clean the tables in a restaurant

d. something used to wipe the mouth or clean the messes

e. a bag used to pack the unfinished dishes

f. a container used for liquids

g. the food that has not been eaten

h. another drink after the first one has been consumed

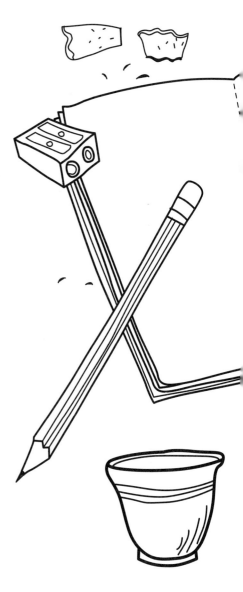

　　如同本單元標題所用的 "tips,"「小費」也可以看成是由 "to insure prompt service"（確保快速服務）所組成的字頭字（acronym）。小費文化在亞洲並不是廣為大家所接受的作法（practice），但在歐美國家，尤其是美國，服務業的薪資（wage）低廉；養家活口（bring home the bacon）就非得靠小費收入了！

　　一般狀況下，旅館的 bellman 或機場車站的 porter 都是以一件行李一美元的比例來計算；如果是搭乘計程車，通常是車資（fare）的 10%，要不然就是找零的數目相當上述比例，"keep the change"（不用找錢也）是個好方法；若在餐廳，午餐通常是 10-15% 而晚餐有時則會以 20-25% 的比例來計算。就算服務的品質並非一時之選，雖少但還是要給！在 2013 年，美國餐飲服務業掀起一陣「把愛送出去」（pay it forward）的風潮。網路上有照片為證，一頓 20 幾元的餐點可以留下百元小費！當然每個人留小費的動機不同，但如果他日在國外作客，入境隨俗（do in Rome as Romans do）在所難免。

Unit
10

How would you like it?
烹飪

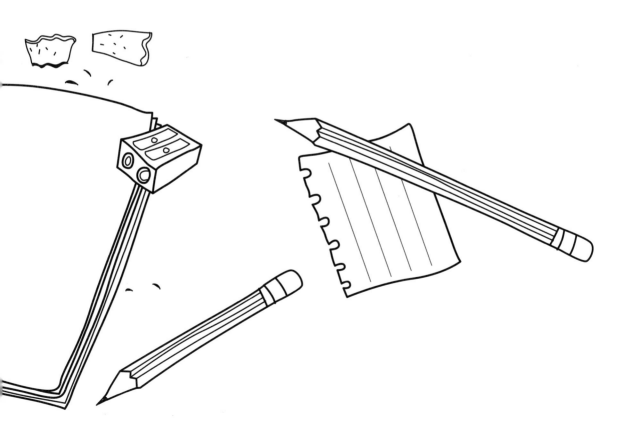

Healthy meals that are also fast can be a challenge (挑戰). With some careful planning you can get healthy meals on the tables in less time too.

Instructions:

1. Plan your meals ahead of time (事先) each week. By planning ahead you can ensure you select quick, and easy recipe (食譜,製作法,烹飪法) that is well balanced (均衡的,明智的).

2. On your grocery (食品雜貨) list be sure to include canned (罐裝) or frozen (冷凍) vegetables along with and fresh ones you are purchasing (購買).

3. Aim to (以…為目標) cook extra so that you can use the leftovers for other meals.

4. Consider making a convenient meal, that is also a family favorite (最喜歡的) once a week. This is a great tip for times of the years when you have plans most evenings. Good choices here may be pizza or lasagna (千層麵) from the frozen food aisle (排列冷凍食品的通道). Add a salad and you have a great meal, quick and easy.

5. Build around (以…為中心) already cooked (煮熟的) meats. Purchase cooked meats by the pound at your local barbeque restaurant. Cook the canned or frozen veggies

(蔬菜) and viola (莖葉蔬菜) and you are done with dinner!

6. Make use of crockpot (慢鍋) cooking. This has become popular again. With a quick search on the internet you will find a number of meals ideas via (經由, 憑藉) your handy (方便的) crock pot.

If you are in a hurry (趕時間), you can still prepare a meal in less than minutes that your whole family will enjoy. All you need is some basic information on nutrition (營養) and a little leap of faith (有信心):

Instructions:

1. Make sure that you have protein (蛋白質), grains (穀類) and vegetables on hand. You can put any combination of these and some appropriate seasonings (調味料, 香料) in a 9-by-12 (9 乘 12) inch (吋) baking pan (烤盤) and prepare a quick casserole (砂鍋) dish.

2. Grab a can. Opening a can is the quickest way to prepare any meal. Some canned foods are a little boring (無趣) but can be spruced up (打扮) with high-flavor (味道香) foods such as a salsa (墨西哥菜中用番茄和辣椒製成的醬汁) to give them a boost (幫助). Try olive (橄欖), corn and tomatoes, which seem to keep most of their flavor and

texture (質地).

3. Try couscous (北非粗麥粉). Couscous is a small pasta-type (麵團) pre-cooks (熟的) grain that takes less than 2 minutes of preparation time to make. Juts boil water, and pour it over the couscous. Add a bit of oil and let it (擱置) for a few minutes. Here you have an instant side dish (小菜). For even less preparation, try pouring couscous and water in with some meat and vegetables and bake them all together. Couscous is very forgiving (寬大 , 隨和) and will absorb (吸收) extra juices from the baking meat.

4. Ensure your protein is easy to prepare by buying individually frozen pieces of meat. For most types of meat, you can place them still frozen into your oven. Just be sure to increase the baking time and check their temperature before serving your meal. Chicken should be at 170 degrees and beef should register (顯示) 160 degrees Fahrenheit (71 Celsius). Also remember cheese and yogurt are protein too and are excellent for making fast meals.

5. Don't be afraid to try new things. The beauty of being a house chef is that you get to (開始) experiment. If the recipe calls for one thing and you don't have it, prepare it with another. For instance, you can substitute one kind of vegetable for another in most meals, and it probably won't affect the end result that much. Your family may even like it better.

Glossary: Words you can use 詞彙

─────── ○ ───────

Cooking terms　烹飪方式

barbequed/grilled	烤，燒 (將食物至於炭火或開放式的熱源上烹調)
baked	烘
casserole	砂鍋
boiled	水煮
braised	燒，燜
braised with soy sauce	紅燒
broil	高溫烤
fried	炒
fried-simmered	扒
pan-fried	煎
roasted	燒臘
sauté	煎
simmered	燉，煨
smoked	燻
steamed	蒸
stewed	燉，煲，燜
stewed in gravy	滷 (gravy: 醬汁、肉汁)
stir-fried/quick-fried	翻炒
twice-cooked stir-frying	回鍋

Ways of preparing ingredients　準備方式

beat	搗成糊狀 (蛋)
break	打破，折斷

chop	剁（碎）
crush	壓碎
cut	切（碎）
dice	切丁
end	根，端
grate	刨絲
grind	磨，碾
julienne	切絲
mash	磨成糊狀（馬鈴薯）
peel	剝皮，削皮
scrub	刷
shell	剝殼
shred	切條
slice	切成薄片
soak	浸
split	切開
squeeze	擠
stir	攪拌
trim	修剪

flavors　味道

acrid	澀的
bitter	苦的
crisp	脆的
greasy	油膩的

heavy	味重的
hot	辣的
insipid	無味的
light	淡的
milder	溫和的
pungent	辛辣的
rich	味濃的
salty	鹹的
sour	酸的
spicy	有香料的
sweet	甜的
starchy	糊的
tender	嫩的
tough	老的

——○——

cantaloupe	甜瓜
drain	排水管
ground	磨碎的
mixture	混合物
review	評論
sink	水池，水槽
sprinkle	撒
spring onion	青蔥
stop up	塞住，堵住
stopper	塞子
trim	修剪

What to Say 情境對話

---○---

Situational Dialogue 1 ☉ 10-1

(Knocking on the door)

R (Room Service): Good evening sir. This is Room Service. May I come in?

G (Guest): Certainly. Come right in.

R Here is your meal. Shall I put it on the table?

G Yes, please. Thank you.

R This is your lobster and king salmon, and here is your clam chowder soup.

G They sure look delicious.

R Would you prefer tartar sauce or Japanese dressing for your lobster and salmon?

G Japanese dressing is lighter, right?

R Yes it's mainly made of lime juice, vinegar and soy sauce.

G Then I'll try it.

Situational Dialogue 2 ☉ 10-2

G What's this? Did I order it?

R That is the fried oysters. You ordered fried oysters, didn't you?

G Oh, yes. That's right.

R Here is the sauce for the oysters. And this is your wine. It's well balanced

and goes well with your lobster.

G Good.

R Shall I open it for you now?

G Yes, please.

R Here is the check and I need you to sign for it. Enjoy your meal.

Situational Dialogue 3　　　　　　　　　　　　　🔅 10-3

S/C (Sous-chef 三廚): What are we going to do?

C (Chef): We are going to make tomato soup.

S/C What should we start with?

C The spring onions.

S/C What should I do?

C Wash the spring onions first. Before you wash the spring onions in the sink, stop up the drain with the stopper. Then trim off both ends. Split the spring onions down the middle with your cook's knife.

S/C OK. I've done that. What should I do next?

C Get me four finely diced tomatoes.

S/C So we are making tomato soup with spring onions.

C That's correct.

Situational Dialogue 4

S/C Are we going to make a fruit salad today?

C Yes. Let's make an orange yogurt dressing first. Give me the oranges.

S/C Yes. How will we prepare the oranges?

C First, we'll squeeze the oranges and then mix the orange juice with oil.

S/C And after that?

C Keep stirring the mixture. That's for the dressing.

S/C I see. It smells good.

C Next, peel the apples, peaches, and cantaloupes. Then you dice them.

S/C And put the dressing on the fruit salad?

C Right.

How to Say It 句型介紹

———○———

- May I serve the ____ now?

- There is a ___ (例：warmer 保溫器) on the cart (推車). Please help yourself, but be careful because it is hot.

- It's a ___ (例：mixture/combination...) of ___ and ___ (例：pepper and various spices). It should be ___ (例：sprinkle) on you food.

- Please put a little of ___ (例：ground mustard) in the ___ (例：soy sauce), mix it, and then dip raw fish in it before eating.

- Please do not eat ___ (例：the leaf by the fish). It's for decoration.

- Use ___ (例：bright colors) to make the salad look nice.

- Add the ___ (例：dressing) to the salad before it is served.

- Use the ___ (例：the outer leaves) for décor.

- Please cut ___ (例：the inner leaves) into bite size piece.

- Wash the ___ (例：plum).
  Soak the ___ (例：grapes).
  Peel the ___. (例：oranges.)
  Slice open the ___. (例：watermelon).
  Remove the seeds from the ___ (例：papaya).
  Serve ___ (例：pineapple) with ice cream.

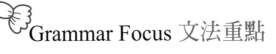

Grammar Focus 文法重點

———○———

在本單元對話中出現了附加問句：

用法：肯定敘述句用否定附加問句，否定敘述句用肯定附加問句

This restaurant is very popular in the city, isn't it?

This restaurant isn't as good as the review said, is it?

注意：小心具有否定意思的字如： no, never, nothing, seldom, little/few, scarcely, hardly,...

There is no such a thing as a free lunch, is it?

He hardly smiles when there is girl present, does he?

例句：

The food has been served, hasn't it?

You had better go to check the customers, hadn't you?

We had to help the new waiter, didn't we?

There is someone in the restroom, isn't there?

These are good recipes, aren't they?

Working and studying at the same time are not easy, are they?

Let's do it, shall we?

Let us leave, will you?

Let's not tell him, all right?

Pass me the sugar, will you?

Have a cup of coffee, won't you?

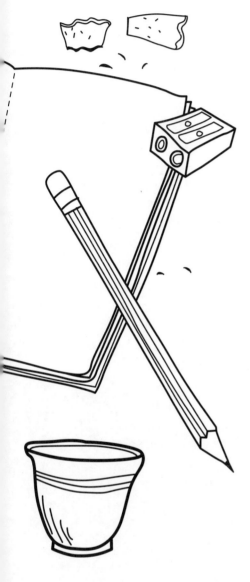

Drills & Exercises

—— 練習 ——

1. Circle the proper words.

   Don't crush/grind this box. There are flowers in-side.

   She crushes/grinds fresh coffee beans every day.

   First, trim/scrub off the ends of the spring onions.

   I want you to dice/cut the green peppers open.

   Now, remove/shell the seeds of the red peppers.

   Please scrub/peel the garlic, and then chop/open it into fine (細小) pieces.

2. Pick out the word which has a different meaning from the other words.

   ____ a. order   b. charge   c. serving   d. portion

   ____ a. enough   b. additional   c. extra   d. plus

   ____ a. be thankful   b. be grateful   c. be careful
   d. be appreciative

   ____ a. send   b. deliver   c. finish   d. bring

   ____ a. bill   b. note   c. paper money   d. coin

3. Choose the word that has a similar meaning with the italic word or phrase.

   ____ What would you *prefer*, tea or coffee?

   (a. drink   b. care   c. like   d. insist)

____ What *kind/kinds* of coffee you have?

(a.type/types   b. brand/brands   c. name/names
d. cup/cups)

____ Would you prefer butter or *jam*?

(a.toast   b. marmalade   c. milk   d. fruit)

____ Would you *care for* something to drink?

(a.order   b. cook   c. like   d. ignore)

____ Could you *say that again*?

(a. return that   b. repeat that   c. rewrite that
d. renew that)

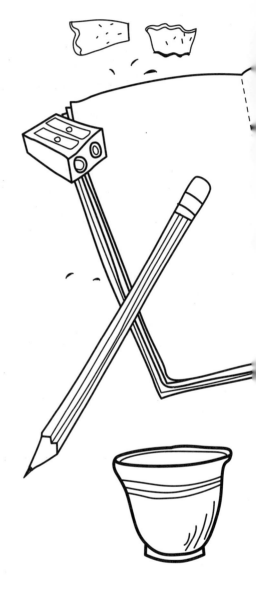

　　如何將中國菜解釋給外國朋友聽可能是個大挑戰，尤其是當外國朋友不熟悉中國菜中所有類別時。

　　一般而言，中國菜大概可分成：

1. 四川菜（Sichuan Cuisine）：注重調味（condiments）多用花椒。代表菜：宮保雞丁

2. 山東菜（Shandong Cuisine）：以爆（quick fry）、炒（stir-fry）、炸（deep-fry），扒（frying and simmering）見長。代表菜：蔥燒海參

3. 廣東菜（Cantonese Cuisine）：以清鮮（light and clear）、爽口（tasty and refreshing）為代表。代表菜：糖醋咕咾肉

4. 江蘇菜（Jiangsu Cuisine）：注意配色刀工、精細口味，偏甜、肥而不膩。代表菜：無錫 排骨

5. 福建菜（Fujian Cuisine）：滋味清淡、鮮嫩、色調美觀。代表菜：佛跳牆

6. 湖南菜（Hunan Cuisine）：口味鹹辣（salty and spicy）、油重（oily）。代表菜：炒臘肉

7. 安徽菜（Anhui Cuisine）：精於燒（broil）、燉（stew）、煙燻（smoke）。代表菜：八公山豆腐

8. 浙江菜（Zhejiang Cuisine）：擅長烹調海鮮、河鮮與家禽。代表菜：龍井蝦仁

　　所以，要介紹中國菜還真是件很困難的事呢！

Unit
11

I have a Sweet Tooth！
甜點

Some people will say that life isn't complete without dessert. And even more will say a meal isn't complete without it. Is it a coincidence (巧合) that "desserts" spell backwards is "stressed?" (緊張 , 有壓力的) Maybe not, but capping (結束) dinner with a nice sweet treat (難得的樂事) is something that can uplift (提升 , 振奮) one's mood (心情) after a long day or a below average (水準之下) meal.

Sweetness is main common dominator (支配者) in most desserts consumed (消耗) worldwide, but apart from that, there is hundreds of thousands of variations (變化) and categories that fall into (分成) this meal course (一道菜). Usually served after the last savory (鹹的) dish and before coffee and tea, the sweet course ranges from a simple fruit plate to decently (合適地 , 體面地) rich and calorie-laden (高熱量) chocolate confections (西點 , 糖果). The simplest of desserts actually do not involve any cooking. Sliced apples, seedless grapes and different berries are offered in temperate (溫和) countries while in hot Asian countries tropical (熱帶的) fruit like mango, papaya and melon in restaurant buffets or as an a la carte menu item elaborately (精心 , 精巧的) cut and served in a hollowed (中空的) watermelon. Pineapple and coconut figure (出現) prominently (顯著

地) in countries in the Asia Pacific. On the other end of the colorful spectrum (系列範圍) of dessert are baked cakes, pies and pastries from flaky (薄片呈層狀) buttery (奶油的) French pastries to all American apple pie. Special occasions and holidays are not complete without traditional desserts: Christmas fruit cake (水果蛋糕) Thanksgiving pumpkin pie and Chinese New Year sticky (黏的) rice cake. Weddings, whatever the religions (宗教) is, usually ended with the cutting of a cake shared between the newly married couple together with a glass of champagne. Baked desserts include cookies, crumbles, meringues , tarts and soufflés with variety of flavors like chocolate, fruit, caramel, spices and a lot more. Custard, gelatin and puddings are usually cooked and then chilled (冷凍的) prior to serving. Other stove top (爐上煮) cooking methods include frying (beignets, funnel cakes and Spanish churros served with an extra thick chocolate dip (浸料), boiling (porridges and sweet soup), steaming (sweet dim sum and other Asian sticky rice (糯米) pastries), and poaching (水煮) (fruits like pears and peaches in red wine). Frozen desserts include ice cream, sherbet which can be served on its own or combined with other ingredients like fruits, syrups, nuts and whipped cream.

Innovative (創新的) and exotic (異國的 , 奇特的) restaurants serve unique creations or make a twist (變化) to the otherwise expected dessert. Among these include ice cream tempura (天婦羅), battered (打扁的) and deep fried chocolate bars and pastries made with durian, a strongly odorous (難聞的) fruit that one either loves and runs away from. One dessert that's gaining a lot of media frenzy (狂熱) is ice cream made with, are you ready for this, breast milk (母奶) ! These are surely talked about even after the meal. Raw (生的) desserts, apart from the fresh fruits, sweetened nuts and seeds, are fast gaining popularity among the health food community. These low-glycemic (低升糖), fiber- (纖維) and nutrient-rich (養分充分) confections (西點 , 糖果 , 果醬 , 蜜餞) are modifications (變型) of cooked goods include dehydrated (脫水的) cookies and pies, super food parfaits and puddings, sweetened with honey, coconut or palm sugar

Glossary: Words you can use 詞彙

—— ○ ——

A

aluminum foil	錫箔紙
apple pie ala mode	蘋果派加冰淇淋
award-winning	得獎的
As American as apple pie	像蘋果派一樣的道地美式

B

batter	搗成糊狀
beignet	法式方形甜甜圈
berries	漿果
brownie	布朗尼：小塊濃郁像餅乾的巧克力蛋糕

C

champagne	香檳酒
cake mix	預先準備好的蛋糕材料
churn	攪乳器
cinnamon	肉桂
cocoa	可可
cooking clinic	烹飪教室
cookie sheet	烘烤食物的烤盤
core	去核
cornstarch	玉米澱粉；太白粉
crack	斷裂

crimp	皺褶
crumbles	酥頂，酥粒，烤奶酥粒
crème brulee (=burned/burnt cream)	焦糖布丁
crème caramel	焦糖蛋奶
crust	派皮
cup cake	杯子蛋糕
curdle	凝結
custard	蛋黃派

D

dot	點
durian	榴槤

E

evaporate	蒸發，脫水
(almond) extract	杏仁油

F

fluffy	蓬鬆柔軟的
fondue (=fondu)	起司火鍋
frosting	糖霜
fudge	以巧克力為底的糖漿
funnel cake	用漏斗將麵糊滴入油鍋油炸的鳥巢蛋糕

G

gelatin	吉利丁，洋菜粉；果凍

h

hold	保留

I

If you can't take the heat, stay away from the kitchen!	不能碰就別摸！

L

layered	分層的
ladyfingers	手指餅乾
literally	就字面而言

M

macaron	馬卡龍：法式小圓餅
mascarpone cheese	馬仕卡彭起司 (類似優酪乳的未熟成起司)
madeleine	法式小型心形飛碟形蛋糕
meringues	蛋白酥
mousse	多泡沫含奶油的甜點：慕斯

N

now that	既然
nutmeg	肉豆蔻

O

overlapping	重疊，交搭

P

panna cotta (= Italian cooked cream)	義式奶酪
pie tin	餡餅烤盤
porridge	燕麥粥
pound cake	磅餅；以一磅糖，奶油和麵粉製成的蛋糕
pudding	布丁

R

rice cake	年糕

S

scoop	勺
scrumptious	絕妙的
shed some light on	闡述，說明
sherbet	類似冰淇淋的果汁或糖類冰品

slit	縱切
sorbet	冷凍果子露
soufflés	舒芙蕾，烤奶酥
Spanish churros	西班牙吉拿棒
spices	香料，調味料
sprinkle	撒
starch	澱粉
stuffed	飽，吃撐了
syrup	(楓)糖漿

T

tart	小烘餅，果餡餅
That's the bomb! (=That's awesome!)	棒透的！
thickener	芡粉，勾芡

Y

yogurt	優酪乳
You got as point there	言之有理

W

whipped cream	鮮奶油

What to Say 情境對話

———○———

Situational Dialogue 1 🔘 11-1

S (Server): Can I interest you in some of our award-winning desserts this evening?

G (Guest): I don't know. I am pretty stuffed.

S We're having a special apple pie a la mode and tiramisu tonight. And they are simply fantastic.

G That sure sounds tempting. By the way, I've heard of apple pie as in "As American as apple pie," but apple pie a la mode?

S It's a classic dessert served warm from the oven and topped with a scoop vanilla ice cream.

G That's the bomb!

S I guarantee you that you'll love it once you get a taste of it.

Situational Dialogue 2 🔘 11-2

G What about tiramisu? Care to shed some light?

S Tiramisu can be translated, literally, into "pick me up" or "lift me up." It's a popular coffee-flavored Italian dessert.

G Is that so?

S It is made of ladyfingers dipped in coffee, layered with a whipped mixture of egg yolks, egg whites, sugar and mascarpone cheese, flavored with cocoa.

G That must be very rich, isn't it?

S It sure is, but who's counting the calories?

G You have a point there; if you can't take the heat, stay away from the kitchen.

G I guess I'll give the apple pie a la mode a try.

S You won't be sorry.

Situational Dialogue 3

 11-3

(In a cooking clinic)

I (Instructor): Today we're going to learn how to bake an apple pie.

S (Student): Is there anything we need to know before we start?

I Make sure to use a good baking apple so that the apples will hold the shape after they are cooked.

S We are all set.

I Good, First, preheat the oven to 425 degrees Fahrenheit. Then, peel, core and slice the apples to 1/2" to 3/4" thick slices and place in a large bowl.

S Then what?

I Mix cinnamon, sugar, cornstarch and nutmeg together and sprinkle over the apples.

I After that, place 1 crust in the bottom of a pie tin, overlapping the edges of pie tin. Pour the sliced apples mixture on crust. Dot apple mixture with butter. Cover the apples with the remaining crust.

Situational Dialogue 4

 11-4

S Now that we have the pie crust ready. What's next?

I Crimp the top crust to the bottom crust. Cut approximately 6 slits in the top crust. To prevent the crimped crust from over browning, cover crimped edges with aluminum foil.

S Mm.

I Place the pie pan on a cookie sheet and place it in the oven. Bake it for 50-60 minutes or until the crust is golden in color and the apples are soft. Serve warm or cold with your favorite topping.

How to Say It 句型介紹

———○———

- 詢問

  Can I interest you with some...?

  Can I interest you in...?

  Can I tempt you with ...?

  Have you heard about ...?

  How about ...?

  Would you care for some ...?

- 說明

  You can substitute ... with...

  You can have ... instead.

  We can hold ... for you if that's too ... (strong, sweet, hot,...).

  Sorry, but we are out of ...

  Unfortunately, we don't have ... in stock right now.

  I'm afraid that we don't serve ... anymore.

  The ... (hot fudge, caramel,...) is very ... (rich, creamy, scrumptious,...)

- 表明己見

  I kind of had my heart set on ...

  I'm determined to have ... for sure.

  I've got to give ... a try.

Grammar Focus 文法重點

———○———

> 在對話中有 "as American as apple pie" 的用法。
>
> As + adj./adv. + as 是個英文中常出現的句型：

▶ So many Asian restaurants have opened up in LA that a writer on a daily paper here jokes that dim sum, Japanese sushi and Vietnamese spring rolls have become as American as apple pie.

洛杉磯地區開了那麼多亞洲餐館，一家日報記者開玩笑地說：「廣東點心、日本壽司和越南春捲」都已經成為像蘋果派一樣的美國食物了。

▶ Football and baseball are as American as apple pie. These two games were invented by Americans and played and watched everywhere in this country. Many people sit glue to their TV sets whenever there are major competitions.

因為它們是美國人發明的，全國各地都有人打和看這兩種球，而且每當有重大比賽時，許多人就坐在電視機前動都不動，所以橄欖球和棒球是美國式的運動。

中國學生很歡說 "as possible as;" 實際上，這種用法並不存在：

Please come here as possible as you can. (✕)
Please come here as soon as possible. (○)

I want to spend as much time as I can with you.
The boy runs as fast as anybody else in his class.

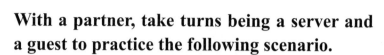

Drills & Exercises

—— 練習 ——

With a partner, take turns being a server and a guest to practice the following scenario.

- A server asks a guest if he or she would like to order dessert. Make a suggestion to encourage the guest to order by using:

  ____ is something to die for.

  The taste of ____ is out of this world!

  Our ____ has been rated as "a must" in town. You have to try it.

  Our award-winning ____ is a treat you have to have.

- As a guest, use the following expressions to learn more about the dessert recommended:

  Is the ____ delicious?

  Do you recommend ____?

  What is ____?

  What are ingredients in it?

  Is ____ ____ (sweet, soft, crunchy,...)?

　　諺語在英文表達中一直扮演著重要的腳色；要能生動有趣且貼切，諺語使用是否得當是個不可或缺的技巧：

- Haste makes waste 欲速則不達
- An idle youth, a needy age 少壯不努力老大徒傷悲
- Two heads are always better than one 三個臭皮匠勝過一個諸葛亮
- No sweet without sweat 苦盡甘來
- Look before you leap 三思而後行
- Bitter medicine has better wholesome effects 良藥苦口
- The journey of a thousand miles starts with one step 萬丈高樓從地起
- Prosperity makes friends; adversity tries them 患難見眞情
- Half loaf is better than no bread 聊勝於無
- Spare the rod spoil the child 棒下出孝子 / 不打不成器
- Too far east is west 矯枉過正
- Practice what you preach 言行一致

　　你還能想出那些日常生活中信手拾來的諺語呢？

Note

Unit 12

Something simple, something light.
速食

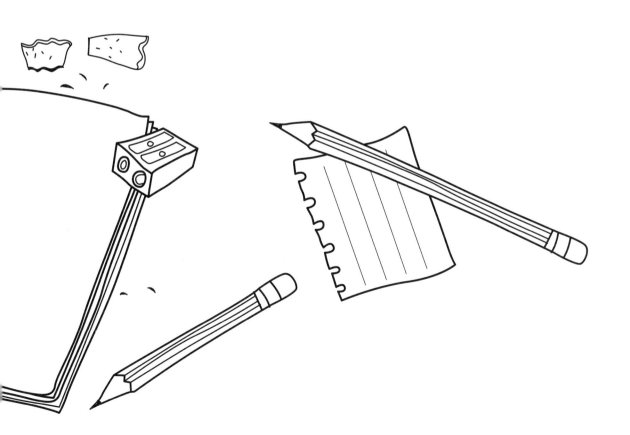

Read 閱讀

Fast food is the term (名稱) given to food that can be prepared and served very quickly. While any meal with low preparation time can be considered as fast food, it is typically a term refers to (談到, 提及) food sold in a restaurant or store with preheated or precooked ingredients, and served to the customers in a packaged form for take-out/take-away (外帶).

Fast food outlets (連鎖店) are take-out or take-away providers, often with "drive-through" (得來速) service that let customers to order and pick up food from their cars, but most also have indoor or outdoor seating areas where customers can eat on-site (現地, 現場). Nearly from its inception (開始, 開端, 啓用), fast food has been designed to be eaten 'on the go' (活躍活動) often does not require cutlery, and is eaten as a finger food. Common menu items at fast food include fish and chips (炸魚和馬鈴薯片), sandwiches, pitas (口袋餅), hamburgers, fried chicken, French fries, onion rings, chicken nuggets, tacos (墨西哥捲餅) pizza, hot dog, and ice cream, though some restaurants offer "slower" food like chili (辣椒肉), mashed potatoes (芋泥) and salads.

Convenience stores located within many petrol/gas stations sell pre-packaged sandwiches, doughnuts (甜甜圈) and hot food. Many gas stations in the United States and Europe also sell frozen foods, and have microwave ovens on the premises (在建築物或周遭土地範圍內) in which to prepare them. Street vendors (攤販) or small or independent operators operating from cart (推車) portable grill (活動烤架) or motor vehicle (food truck, 餐車) are also a part of the fast food scene. Street vendors provide a colorful and varying range of options (選擇) designed to quickly captivate (吸引, 捕捉) passers-by (路人) and attract as much attention as possible.

Depending on the locale (場所, 地點), multiple (複合的多樣的) street vendors may specialize in specific types of food characteristics (特質) of a given cultural or ethnic (民族) tradition. In some cultures, it is typical for street vendors to call out prices, sing or chant (吟誦) sales-pitches (推銷商品的言辭), play music, or engage in other forms of "street theatrics" (街頭藝術表演) to engage prospective (可能的) customers. In some cases, this can garner (獲得) more attention than the food.

Modern commercial fast food is often highly processed (處理過的) and prepared in an industrial fashion (方式), i.e., on a large scale (規模) with standard ingredients and standardized (標準化的) cooking and production methods. It is usually rapidly served in cartons (紙盒) or in a plastic wrapping (塑膠包裝), in a fashion (方式 , 方法) that minimizes (縮小) cost. In most fast food operations, menu are generally made from processed ingredients prepared (處理過的) at a central supply facility and then shipped to individual outlets where they are reheated, cooked (usually by microwave or deep frying) or assembled (組合) in a short amount of time. This process ensures a consistent level of product quality, and is key to being able to deliver the order quickly to the customers and eliminate (消除) labor and equipment costs in the individual stores.

Other than the ever-popular (廣受歡迎的) kinds of fast food, Chinese take-outs consisting of noodles, rice and meat, Japanese sushi rolled in nori (dried laver 紫菜) with fillings of fish, seafood, chicken or cucumber, Italian pizza, kebab (沙威瑪：捲餅) from the Middle East and fish and chips from the United Kingdom are all becoming the inevitable parts of this fast food map.

Glossary: Words you can use 詞彙

A

apple dippers	蘋果片

B

barbequed	烤肉醬的
biscuit	肯德基的軟餅
BLT (bacon, lettuce and tomato)	培根生菜番茄三明治
bone-in chicken	帶骨雞肉
bone-out chicken	去骨雞肉
bun	小圓麵包

C

central supply facilities	中央廚房
chargrilled	炭烤的
chicken nugget	雞塊
chicken wing	雞翅
chicken strip	雞條，雞柳
chicken wrap	雞肉捲
chop suey	雜碎；什錦
condiment	調味料，佐料
coleslaw	涼拌捲心菜
combo (=combination)	套餐；也有人會說成 meal number...
complimentary	免費的

consistent	一貫的，堅持的

D

dark meat	泛指雞腿、雞翅等部位的雞肉
deck	層 (如用在三層漢堡); stack 層 (如用在鬆餅)
deli (delicatessen)	熟食店
double ___ (cheeseburger)	雙層…

E

egg roll/spring roll	春捲
entrée	主菜
exchange	交談

F

filet-O-fish	魚堡
finger-licking	舔指頭
flame-grilled	火烤的
flurry	陣風：冰炫風
frost	冰霜 (Wendy's 溫蒂漢堡的特製冰品)

G

garner (= earn)	賺到，贏得
grounded ___ (beef, pork...)	絞肉

H

hold (bakc)	取消
honey mustard sauce	蜂蜜芥末醬

J

jumbo	特大杯；medium 中杯

K

ketchup	番茄醬

M

manage	應付，處理
___-marinated	以…醃製的
mayo (mayonnaise)	美乃滋
meat patty	肉餅

N

nag	嘮叨

O

olive	橄欖

P

pickle	醃黃瓜
pottage	濃湯
pot sticker	鍋貼
pressure-cooked	高壓烹調

R

regular	正規尺寸，普通大小
relish	碎黃瓜；開胃小菜
rye	裸麥，黑麥

S

session	（一堂）課
shake	奶昔
straw	吸管
straw dispenser	放置吸管的容器
sub (submarine)	潛艇三明治
sundae	聖代
sweet and sour sauce	糖醋醬

T

thigh	雞腿
tray	托盤
turkey roll	火雞捲 (經過處理的火雞肉)
turkey breast	火雞胸 (未經處理的火雞肉)

W

wheat	小麥
white	白 (麵包)
white meat	泛指雞胸肉
wrap	……捲

What to Say 情境對話

———○———

Situational Dialogue 1 ⊛ 12-1

(In a fast food restaurant)

C1 (Clerk): Can I help the next person in line? How's it going?

C2 (Customer): Pretty good. How about yourself?

C1 Good. What's it going to be today?

C2 One Combo number 3 and one number 5, please.

C1 Anything to drink?

C2 A jumbo diet Coke and one regular iced tea.

C1 By adding 35 cents you can have an extra-large size of fries instead.

C2 Why not? And an extra order of onion rings and one flurry with Oreo cookies.

C1 Is that for here or to go?

C2 For here, please.

Situational Dialogue 2 ⊛ 12-2

(In a deli/delicatessen)

C1 Can I help you?

C2 A BLT on rye with everything and a turkey breast on white with extra lettuce and tomato but hold the mayo.

C1 What kind of cheese?

C2 American cheese for both.

C1 How about something to drink?

C2 One apple juice and one mineral water. The sandwiches come with chips, right?

C1 Yes. What flavor?

C2 Barbeque for both.

Situational Dialogue 3   12-3

M (Mother): John, aren't you going to have your lunch before you go to school?

J (John): I don't have time. I'm already late for class.

M But it's a three-hour session; can you manage without something to eat?

J I don't think I have too much of a choice.

M Why don't you grab a bite on the run? There's a sandwich shop on the way.

J I guess I could. I wish I had managed my time better.

M Well, it's never too late to learn.

J OK, mom, stop nagging me.

Situational Dialogue 4

(In a Chinese take-out)

C1 For 3.95, you can have either fried rice or chow mein plus two entrees; and for 5.95, you can have either steamed rice, fried rice or chow mein plus three choices.

C2 They all look delicious. What's that?

C1 Beef broccoli with oyster sauce. It's finger-licking good! The sweet-and-sour pork is another good choice if you ask me.

C2 I think I'll have them both plus egg rolls.

C1 What kind of rice would you like?

C2 I'll have the steamed rice. And do you provide complimentary soup?

C1 That will cost you an extra 1.50. Today's soup is minced chicken and corn pottage.

C2 I'll pass. Thank you, anyway.

How to Say It 句型介紹

———○———

If you are going to order submarine sandwich (潛艇三明治), the followings are the things you need to decide:

- What would you like?
  I'd like a sub (a salad, or a wrap).

- What type of bread?
  I'd like wheat/white/honey oat (蜂蜜燕麥) /Italian herbs (義式香草) /cheese

- Which size?
  I'd like to have a 6-inch/footlong

- Which extras (額外的)?
  I'd like to double on meat
  I'd like to have it with strips of bacon.

- Which veggies (蔬菜)?
  I'd like to have lettuce/tomato/pickles/cucumber/pepper/red onion/olive/jalapenos (墨西哥辣椒)

- Which sauce (佐料醬)?
  I'd like to have the sweet onion/honey mustard/sweet chili/Italian/ranch/thousand island/barbeque

- Make it a meal (正餐)?
  I'd like to have it paired with (搭配) side (chocolate cookies) and a drink

If you are order at a McDonald's, you might want to use the followings:

- Ordering Coffee:
  What size?

Do you want that hot or iced?

Do you want cream or sugar/equal (代糖)?

= Hi, can I please have a medium coffee with 2 creams and 2 sugars?

- Ordering Happy Meals:

Cheeseburgers, hamburgers, or nuggets?

Do you want a regular Happy Meal or the Mighty Kids' Meal?

French fries or apple dippers?

What do you want to drink?

= Hi, can I have a cheeseburger Happy Meal with apple dippers (蘋果片沾醬) and a chocolate milk to drink?

- Ordering Value Meals (經濟餐):

What size

What number it is?

What do you want to drink?

= Hi, can I have a medium number 3 with a Coke?

- Ordering McNuggets:

How many do you want?

Do you want them in a Happy Meal?

= Hi, can I have a 6-piece McNugget with Sweetn' Sour sauce?

- Ordering French fried:

What size?

Do you want salt?

= Hi, can I have medium fries with no salt?

Grammar Focus 文法重點

在速食店點餐時，免不了會用到形容詞如 large/medium/small 等字眼來形容。使用不同形容詞時的次序為何呢？

冠詞 + 所有格 + 指示形容詞 (this/that, these/those) + 不定形容詞 (some, any,...) + 數量 + 性質 + 大小 + 長短 + 新舊 + 顏色 + 專有形容詞 (Chinese/Japanese,...) + 材料

It is a small Japanese wooden bowl.

That tall old English gentleman is a professor.

I would like to have an iced venti (特大杯)caramel (焦糖) frappuccino.

副詞在修飾動詞、形容詞或副詞時，也有先後順序的習慣：
當兩個以上的同種類的副詞修飾同一對象時，依小單位 + 大單位的順序排列

I was born on April 16 in 1991.

My address is at No. 70 on Ta-chih Street in Taipei.

若是不同種類的副詞，則依 (1) 地方 + 時間，(2) 地方 + 時間 + 方法及 (3) 狀態 + 地方 + 時間的順序

My father returned home by air yesterday.

She sang beautifully at the party last night.

Drills & Exercises

——練習——

Work with a partner and take turns as a server and a customer to use the steps provided in the "How to Say It" section to practice ordering food at different fast food outlets:

A Chinese take-out restaurant

A coffee shop

A hamburger joint

An exchange in a hamburger joint can be like this:

Server: What's going to be today?

Customer: I'd like to order ....

Server: How about something to drink?

Customer: I want ....

Server: Will there be anything else?

Customer: I would also like to have ...

Server: Is it for here or to go?

Customer: It's ...

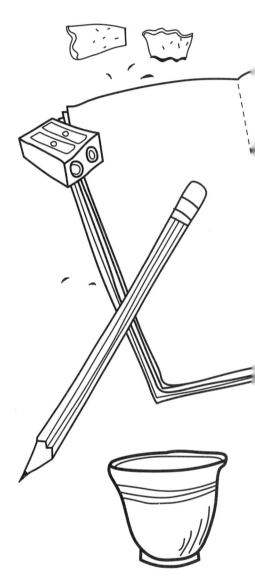

　　美國紐約市新市長 Bill de Blasio 在剛上任就讓自己上了報紙的頭條；他用刀叉吃披薩！除了大家想要看政治人物出糗的心態外，這則新聞點出另一個重點：那些食物要用餐具，而那些食物又能用手吃呢？

　　漢堡通常是油且多汁（greasy and juicy），所以用餐具（kitchen utensil）似乎是正確的選擇，尤其是吃到一半，漢堡下部的麵包（the bottom half of the bun）會變濕（soaky），用手真麻煩！但是用刀叉，想要去切小塊的漢堡也不是件容易事。一般作法是用刀將漢堡包壓緊讓肉汁留在肉餅裡，然後在輕輕切下一能用叉子叉起來大小的漢堡送入嘴中。

　　炸雞是另一個挑戰；棒棒腿（drumstick）或雞翅（wing）通常不會有狀況，因為我們都是用手拿著吃，較難切割的是雞腿（thighs）和雞胸（breasts）。一般作法是將雞肉切成一口的大小，而在切的同時也可將脆（crispy）的皮和嫩（tender）的肉同時切下；就算無法兩全其美，至少有餐具，你還能將分開的雞肉和脆皮同時用刀叉拾起並送入口中。相形之下，若用手很可能讓自己變得很「骯髒」（messy）！

　　中國人的筷子還是強過西洋人的刀叉，不是嗎？

Unit

13

Over-charged and under-served！
抱怨

Read 閱讀

Handling complaints is a vital (重要的) of customer service, whether you work for a fast-food restaurant or a five-star hotel. Addressing (針對) these complaints properly is key when it comes to (想起,談到) protecting your company's reputation and keeping customers coming back, but it is just as important that you learn what makes people complain in the first place. Finding out what makes customers complain can help to prevent (防止) future complaints, saving you time and keeping your customers happier.

False promises (虛假的承諾)

One of the most common sources of complaints occurs when a customer feels that he or she was promised something and the company did not follow through (堅持到底). For example, your company's Web site might claim (聲稱) that you ship out (運出) all orders (訂單) within 24 hours, but since you've been understaffed (員工不足), it might take two days to ship now. In order to prevent these sorts of complaints, be sure to occasionally (不時) check your Web site and your advertisements to make sure that you are still able to offer hat is promised.

Poor-quality product (品質惡劣的產品)

Not everyone is going to be satisfied with the product or service you are selling, no matter how great it is. However, if you are receiving multiple (多樣的) complaints about a product not working, it might be time to start checking your stock (庫存) and testing the item yourself. Making all the sales in the world won't help your business if what you're selling is subpar (水準之下).

Failure to keep up to date (進度落後)

When a customer gets in contact with you, especially when it involves a previous complaint, taking days to get back to them will only make it worse. Even if (就算), for example, you are facing a delay on shipping a package out, the correct thing to do is to send an email or make a phone call, letting customer know. Keeping your customers up to date is an easy way to let them know you care about the business.

Bad service (壞服務)

Poor customer service can cause complaints for a variety of reasons. It might be having a less-than-gracious (無禮的) attitude, failing to answer the phone or chatting with co-workers while ignoring (忽略) customers standing nearby

(附近). These complaints are very preventable (可防止的), for the most part (絕大部分). You need to know the importance of how your customer service is perceived (為他人所感覺到的), provided proper training and keep those who don't have a proper attitude away from the customers.

In the customer service world, not every complaint is warranted (合理的), but taking note (紀錄) of every complain will help you improve your service over time (隨著時間). Learning why people complain can help you to anticipate (預期) complaints before they happen, saving you time, retaining (保留 , 維持) the customers you already have and attracting additional business.

Glossary: Words you can use 詞彙

———○———

- 桌面擺設

  a filthy/dirty/untidy tablecloth 骯髒的

  a ... (wine) stain 有…漬

  a ... (chipped, cracked, dented) …有缺角，破裂，凹痕的…

  a ... (fly, cockroach) in my ... (soup, drink) 蒼蠅，蟑螂

  a ... (chair, table) with ... (a wobbly leg) 搖晃的

  a ... (long wait, bad attitude, slow/sloppy service, ignorant waiter)

- 烹飪方式

  The ... is ... too milder/tasteless 淡味

  　　　　　too hot 辣

  　　　　　spicy 香料太多

  　　　　　salty 鹹

  　　　　　sour 酸

  　　　　　bitter 苦的

  　　　　　greasy 油膩的

  　　　　　heavy 味重的

  　　　　　rich 油膩的

  　　　　　pungent 辛辣的

  　　　　　plain/insipid 無味的

  　　　　　tough/overcooked 老的

  　　　　　raw/rare/undercooked 生的

  (牛排要多熟：rare 三分熟，medium-rare 四分熟，medium 五分熟，medium-well 七八分熟，well-done 全熟)

  　　　　　acrid 澀的

  　　　　　starchy 糊的

A

| absurd | 荒謬，不合理的 |

B

| be fed up with | 受夠了 |
| be sick of | 厭倦 |

C

| cockroach | 蟑螂 |

E

| fail to | 未能 |
| excuse | 藉口 |

F

| flat | 沒氣了 |

G

| gravy | 肉汁，醬料 |

H

| hostess | 女招待 / 迎賓員 |

I

ignorant	無知的

K

keep ... up to date	保持近況

L

look into	調查

M

make up for	補償
misunderstanding	誤會
mix-up/screw-up	混亂，搞砸

N

nowhere to be seen/found	找不到

O

on top of	在…上面
on the side	在…旁邊
originally	當初，原先地

R

realize	理解，了解
replace	更換、代替
ridiculous	無法理解的

S

sloppy	馬虎的，草率的
specific	明確的

T

take it	猜
ticket	點菜單
turn out	結果是…
to get ...for free/out of charge = to get a complimentary ...	免費的…

W

way too + adj.	太…
(you) see	你知道…，要知道…

What to Say 情境對話

Situational Dialogue 1

🔘 13-1

G (Guest): Waiter!

S (Server): Yes, sir?

G I've been trying to catch your attention for the last 15 minutes.

S I'm sorry, sir. Is there anything you need?

G How much longer are we going to have to wait for our dinner?

S I'm afraid the roasted duck takes quite a while to prepare. I'll check it for you right away. In the meantime, would you care for another drink?

G That won't be necessary.

Situational Dialogue 2

🔘 13-2

S Is everything to your satisfaction?

G No, as a matter of fact. The duck isn't as crispy as you originally recommended, the champagne is flat, and we asked specifically to have the sauce on the side but it was on the top instead; in short, nothing seems to be right!

S I'm sorry to hear that. I apologize for all the mix-ups. I'll replace your drink right away and check with the kitchen to see if there is anything we can do.

G To be honest, I didn't expect things would turn out to be like this. I must say I am very disappointed!

S I can definitely understand how you feel, sir. Again, I am really sorry about all the screw-ups.

Situational Dialogue 3 13-3

M (Manager): Good evening, sir. My name is John and I am the manager here. I just want to find out how your evening is so far?

G (Guest): Everything would be fine except our server is nowhere to be found!

M I'm sorry to hear that, but we have been extremely busy tonight. It's Chinese New Year's eve, you know.

G That sounds like an excuse to me!

M Yes, you're quite right. No matter what, there's no excuse for you to be treated like this. Can I take your order for you?

G Sure. I'll have the House Fried Seafood Platter and my lady friend will have the Catch of the Day. We both will have mashed potatoes with gravy.

M I'll place your order with the kitchen right away.

G One more thing. When we first got here, I left a package with your hostess, and she said she'd bring it to our table.

M I take it she never did.

G That's correct.

M Allow me to look into this for you.

Situational Dialogue 4

13-4

C (Chef): You do realize that, as a server, you are supposed to bring the food out, not bring it back to the kitchen.

S (Server): I know, chef, but the steak for Table 5 is overcooked. It was supposed to be medium-well.

C OK, we'll prepare a new one for him. What else are you holding there?

S It's Today's Special. The lady at Table 9 said it's not the way she wanted it.

C You have to be more specific. How did she want it?

S She asked to have the sauce on the side.

C Here's your ticket and you didn't mention it.

S I'm sorry, and I'll be more careful next time.

C Fine, alright. Tell her that her order will be ready in 5 minutes.

How to Say It 句型介紹

———○———

- 表示不滿

    Oh, dear!

    Oh, no!

    I can't believe it!

    Why does that always happen!

    For goodness/haven's/Pete's/pity's/God's sake!

- 表達極端不滿

But that's (absolutely)	ridiculous!	
	outrageous!	
	absurd!	
	unfair!	
	unacceptable!	
	unreasonable!	
It's just/simply	not fair to	charge us for the ...!

- 表示無法接受

    Well I don't think it's fair to make us pay for.....

    Well I have to say that the service was pretty slow, so I don't really feel like leaving a tip.

    Well, there was a cockroach in my ... and the ...wasn't the way I wanted it.

    Well, actually, I don't think you should charge us for ...

    I think you should give us the ...for free, actually.

- 表示對某事的無法苟同

    I'm fed up with .....!

    I'm sick of .....!

    I'm tired of ....!

    I'm sick and tired of ....!

I hate the way you ....!
I can't stand the way you ....!
What really gets under my skin is ....!
What really drives me crazy is ....!

● 道歉

I'm really sorry for/about ....
I'd like to apologize for ....

● 接受對方道歉

That's OK.
No problem.
Don't worry about it.
No worries.

Note

Grammar Focus 文法重點

在本單元對話中出現了現在完成進行式 "I have been trying to catch your attention" 的用法。

現在完成式和現在完成進行式除了在句型上書寫不同之外，

現在完成式 S + have/has + p.p.
現在完成進行式 S + have/has + been + V-ing

它們之間更代表不同的時間長度。

現在完成式表示某一動作自過去某時開始，到現在說話同時結束：
I have studied English for 10 years (and I am not going to study it any more).

現在完成式則代表某一動作自過去某點時間開始，進行到現在說話的時間，而且會持續到未來：
I have been studying English for 10 years (and I will continue studying it in the future).

在使用動詞時態時，一定要注意到不同時態之間所有的些許差異，否則容易造成聽者認知上的誤解。

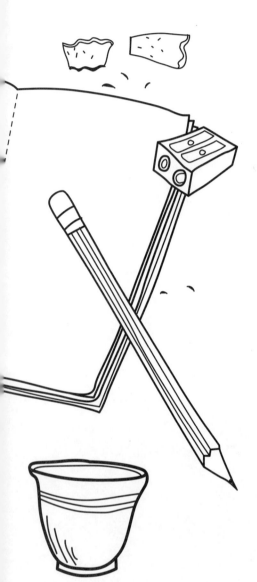

—— 練習 ——

Work with a partner and practice conversations between a server and a customer by using the expressions provided:

Complaints:

- How much longer shall I wait for my...?

- You've been ignoring us all evening. We've finished our dinner 20 minutes ago.

- I ordered a ... but got a ...instead.

- I specifically asked for ... since I'm on a diet.

- We made the reservation yesterday. Would you please check again. I'm sure there must be a mistake.

- We didn't order the ..., why is it on the bill?

- The steak is ... (underdone/overcooked/too tough/ too dry)!

- This toast is ... (too dark/too light/burnt/stale/ soggy/damp)

Replies:

- I'm terribly sorry, ma'am. We're short of help today.

- I'm terribly sorry about this, sir. Thank you for bringing the matter to our attention. I'll definitely look into it.

- I'm sorry. I'll change it for you immediately.

- I'm sorry, sir. I'll return your ... to the chef and have him cook it again.

- I'll have them prepare another one. Would you like some ... while you are waiting?

- I'll attend to/take care of this right away.

- There could have been some mistakes. I do apologize.

- To express out regret for all the trouble, we offer you a ...% discount off the bill.

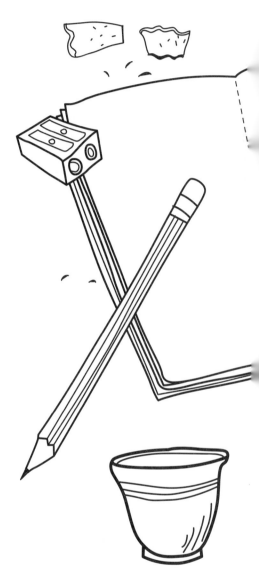

　　如果在餐廳中所接受到不好的待遇（treatment），該是逆來順受（to grin and bear it）還是要表示不滿？而表示不滿，如何做才會有效果？下列的幾個鐵律（cardinal rules）可供參考：

1. Act immediately 立即採取行動
　　息事寧人（to make concession, to stay on good terms）絕非首選！有狀況就該立即反應（to voice out）。

2. Remain calm and objective.
　　切忌情緒化（emotional）；保持冷靜就事論事（to confine the issue to discussion）。

3. Suggest a solution that matches your complaint.
　　提出能化解不滿的解決之道。

4. Take it to the next level.
　　若當場無法得到滿意的回覆，將事情提高到較高層次（to the person in charge）。許多狀況中，因當事人權責不夠而敷衍或打太極拳去淡化（to water down）只會讓事情變得更糟。

5. Reduce the tip or even skip the tip
　　減少甚至不給小費。但若不是當事人的錯，例如菜色中的烹飪技術或手法出了狀況，不要把氣出在服務生身上。

6. Seek outside help
　　消費者基金會（Consumer Foundation）或類似「水果」日報般的八卦報紙（tabloid papers）都是可以申訴的對象。

7. Immediately report any illness.
　　若出了健康狀況或生病了，要立即反應。

　　上述作法雖未必代表事情會有善終，但至少會讓對方知道你是當真（You mean business）；能捍衛自己的權益（be assertive）才是王道（the best way）。

Unit
14

Check, please.

付帳

Read 閱讀

Eating out is one of the life's pleasures (樂事) most of the time. Occasionally, though, the service is poor, the price charged (收取) is not correct, or the food or drink is not up to (未達) quality standards (品質標準). When this happens, you have a right (權利) to dispute (對⋯提出質疑) the restaurant bill and possibly pay less or not at all.

1. Decide if a portion (份量) of the meal does not look right or taste the way it should. You must call the server over right away after having taken a bite (吃一口) so she/he has a chance to correct the problem.
2. Check the bill carefully for accurate (正確的) billing (帳務). If you see a discrepancy (差異), dispute it with the cashier (出納), server or manager while still in the restaurant.
3. Remove additional (額外的) charges (收費) not disclosed (透露, 公開) on the menu or by the server. For example, it is common for restaurants to serve bread with the meal for no additional charge. If the restaurant has a charge for the bread, this should be clearly listed on the menu.
4. Dispute the charge on the restaurant bill even if it is on the menu. If you have never been to this restaurant be-

fore and they charged for bread, even if it is on the menu, if the server does not point it out when you order it, dispute the charge. The next time you back, though, prepare to pay for the bread or do not order it.

5. Pay the bill in full "under protest" (抗議中) if the management does not agree with your dispute. Note on (記載 , 登錄) the bill exactly what you dispute and why. Call the headquarters (總部) for the restaurant when they are available (可得到的), make your complaint and request a refund (退費) of your disputed portion of the bill.

To sum up, when you notice an error with your restaurant bill that you're being overcharged or you may be charged for the wrong item, bring this to the attention (使某人注意) of the waiter what was order and what was charged immediately. If this does not work, as for a manager and explain the dilemma (困境).

Do not feel embarrassed or "swallow the insult" (忍氣吞聲) when you realize that your right has been violated (侵犯), especially when you are the one paying the bill!

Glossary: Words you can use 詞彙

———○———

A

add up to.../come to...	共達…

B

bill/check	帳單
breakdown	細目
business card	名片
by the way	對了；順道一提

C

calculate	計算
cashier	收銀員，出納
cash or charge	現金或刷卡
cash register	收銀機
change	零錢
coupon	折價券
credit card slip	信用卡簽單
credit card transaction machine	信用卡交易機 / 信用卡
credit card terminal	終端機

D

difference	差額
discrepancy	差異，不一致

E

eat the cost	自行吸收
enter	輸入
evenly	平均

F

fat-finger syndrome	手誤，輸入錯誤
foreign/local currency	外幣 / 本地貨幣
foot (V.)	支付

G

generous	慷慨的，大方的
get going	出發，離開
go Dutch	各付各的
gratuity	賞錢，小費

I

ID (identification)	身分證
insert	輸入，鍵入
invoice	發票 (通常使用在生意上)

J

(tip) jar	(放置小費的) 廣口玻璃罐

K

keep the change	不找零

M

match	符合
minimum charge	最低消費

O

on the house	店家請客
overlook	忽略

P

patronage	光臨惠顧
PIN (personal identification number)	個人密碼
press	按，壓

R

receipt	收據
round off	四捨五入

S

separate	分開的

service charge	服務費
settle	支付結算
signature	簽名
skip out (the bill)	偷偷離開
split	分攤
swipe (card)	刷 (卡)
sufficient	(足) 夠了

T

tab	帳款，費用
tips (to insure prompt service)	小費
total (N./V.)	總數：加起來

V

voucher	交換券

What to Say 情境對話

Situational Dialogue 1

14-1

W (Waiter): And how was your meal?

G (Guest): It was wonderful. I think we are ready for our check now.

W Of course. I'll prepare your check right away.

G Thanks. Oh, by the way, my wife ordered a soufflé, but it never came.

W Is that so? I'm terribly sorry that I simply overlooked that. Would you like me to get it for her?

G No, it's getting late and we have to get going. Not to mention we're too full for anything else.

W I understand. I'll make sure not to include it on the bill.

Situational Dialogue 2

14-2

W Here's your bill.

G Thank you. Is the service charge included?

W No, it isn't. I hope you enjoyed your meal.

G It was lovely, thank you.

W Can you put in your PIN and press ENTER? And here's your card and your receipt.

G Thanks. That's for you.

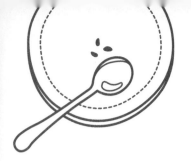

W That's very kind of you. Thank you for your patronage and I hope to see you again soon.

Situational Dialogue 3 14-3

G Excuse me, could you please bring the bill?

W Yes, right away.

W It comes to 70 dollars. Are you paying cash or using a credit card?

G Cash. Here's eighty-five.

W Is this ready to go, Sir?

G Yes, it is. You can keep the change.

W Very kind of you. Thank you for coming.

Situational Dialogue 4 14-4

W Are you ready for your check?

G Yes, I think we are about done with the meal.

W Would you like me to bring you separate checks, or just put everything on one bill?

G One bill will be sufficient. I think we'll split the bill evenly amongst ourselves. By the way, do you accept credit cards?

W Yes, we accept all major credit cards.

G One more question. Do we pay you or at the cash register?

W At the table here. I will be right back with your check.

G I will also need you to put my company's invoice number on the receipt. Here is my business card, and the number is on it.

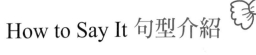

How to Say It 句型介紹

———○———

下列句型和表達可用於和付帳相關的情況中：

- Can I have the bill, please?

- Let me have the check, will you?

- Bring the check, please.

- May I have the bill, please?

- The bill, please.

- It's my treat.

- I'll foot the bill.

- A Dutch treat. = Go Dutch.

- Can I have breakdown of the bill?

- I think there is something wrong with bill.

- I think there are some discrepancies on the bill.

- Is the service charge/tax added to the bill?

- Can we use the voucher/coupon here?

- Can I combine the discount card and coupon/voucher together?

Grammar Focus 文法重點

———○———

"Billing" 帳務和 "bill" 帳單兩者的意思不同，這點出了英文中名詞和動名詞在使用時的差距：

Can I have the bill (帳單)?
All employees need to fill out their time sheet (工作時間紀錄單) so that the accounting department can send the correct billing (帳務) information to clients.

類似的用法：

Jack works in the bank (銀行); he is in the banking business (金融業).

Mary majors in International Trade (國際貿易), and she plans to work for a trading company (貿易公司) after she graduates.

My office does not have enough staffing (人員配置); a staff (工作人員) of 5 can never get all the work done.

名詞通常用來表示靜態的事物或觀念；動名詞則用來表示實際的運作。

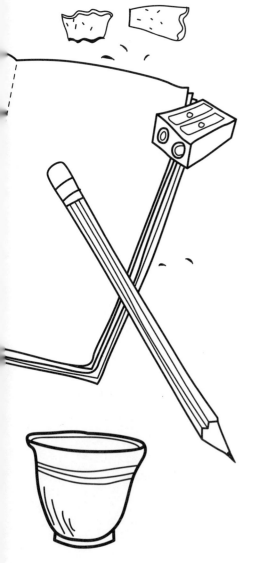

Drills & Exercises

練習

Work with a partner and come up with the correct answers.

1. Server: How would you like to pay for the meal?

    Customer: a. It's my treat.

    b. Go Dutch.

    c. Can I pay it with my credit card?

    d. The food was excellent!

2. Server: Do you need a breakdown of the bill?

    Customer: a. In cash.

    b. By credit card.

    c. Charge it to my room.

    d. A total will be just fine.

3. Customer: a. May I have an invoice?

    b. Can I have a breakdown of the bill?

    c. Does it include all the expenses?

    d. Can I use the voucher?

    Server: Certainly, ma'am. Can I have the name of your company?

4. Customer: That's much more than I expected.

    Server: a. I'm sure that there is no mistake.

    b. Shall I explain some items for you?

    c. Your bill comes to a total of $120.

d. Is that so?

5. Server: Do you want separate bills or just one single bill?

Customer: a. I'll foot the bill.

b. We need clear breakdown of the total.

c. Separate bills, please.

d. She will take care of that.

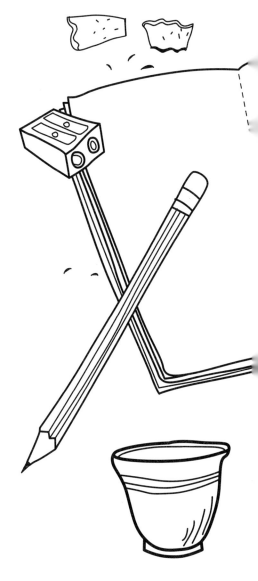

　　自己開餐廳擁有自己的事業；多少人想如此，但多少人卻每每因經營不善而倒閉！不就是吃飯嘛有甚麼難？

　　如果你想要當廚神，下列的錯誤要儘可能避免：

- Not knowing the costs to operate a business.
  食材、庫存、生財、水電房租再加人事；這些都要錢！開餐廳做生意絕非無底洞（money pit），凡事都要精打細算、控制成本。
- Not communicating well with the staff.
  和工作人員之間溝通不良。工作人員是餐廳老闆和客人之間的唯一聯繫，是讓老客人反覆回來的原因，更是餐廳關門大吉的致命傷！
- Not training staff properly
  未能充分訓練員工。不論內場或外場，不管事廚師或跑堂，沒有訓練或是訓練錯誤都會對餐廳的存活有莫大的影響。
- Not listening to customers.
  不能接受客人的建議。迷信專業執意孤行，但卻忽略了能真正左右餐廳運作的客人的建議或回饋；在此情境下，沒有任何餐廳能存活。
- Not willing to change.
  不能隨這趨勢潮流做改變。不是要沒有原則隨波逐流（to go with the flow），但至少要能合乎主流文化（social/cultural mainstream）而做修正（modifications）。

　　當自己的主宰，圓自己的夢；不知修正改進，絕不可能萬年長青、永續經營的！

國家圖書館出版品預行編目資料

餐飲英語／李普生著.
－－初版.－－臺北市：五南, 2014.07
　面；　公分
ISBN 978-957-11-7651-2 (平裝)
1.英語　2.餐飲業　3.讀本
805.18　　　　　　　　　103009396

1AH3

餐飲英語

作　　者 ─ 李普生

發 行 人 ─ 楊榮川

總 編 輯 ─ 王翠華

主　　編 ─ 朱曉蘋

封面設計 ─ 童安安

出 版 者 ─ 五南圖書出版股份有限公司

地　　址：106台北市大安區和平東路二段339號4樓

電　　話：(02)2705-5066　　傳　　真：(02)2706-6100

網　　址：http://www.wunan.com.tw

電子郵件：wunan@wunan.com.tw

劃撥帳號：01068953

戶　　名：五南圖書出版股份有限公司

台中市駐區辦公室/台中市中區中山路6號

電　　話：(04)2223-0891　　傳　　真：(04)2223-3549

高雄市駐區辦公室/高雄市新興區中山一路290號

電　　話：(07)2358-702　　傳　　真：(07)2350-236

法律顧問　林勝安律師事務所　林勝安律師

出版日期　2014年7月初版一刷

定　　價　新臺幣320元